PEN PALS:
BOOK EIGHT

SEALED
WITH A KISS

by Sharon Dennis Wyeth

A YEARLING BOOK

Published by
Dell Publishing
a division of
Bantam Doubleday Dell Publishing Group, Inc.
666 Fifth Avenue
New York, New York 10103

The trademark Yearling ® is registered in the U.S. Patent and Trademark
Office.

ISBN: 0-440-40272-7
Published by arrangement with Parachute Press, Inc.
Printed in the United States of America
March 1990
10 9 8 7 6 5 4 3 2 1
OPM

For Gina

CHAPTER ONE

Dear Lisa,
   I said I'd give you the shirt off my back, and here it is.
Anyway a piece of it—just what you asked for—though I
still can't figure out what you're going to do with it. But
mine is not to reason why, not where Alma Stephens girls are
concerned.
   How are you? I'd like to say I wish you were here, but I
wouldn't wish being at old "Ard-barf" Academy on any-
body right now. The instructors are really into torturing us.

Yes—that's torturing *not* tutoring. *It seems like I have a test or a paper due every other day. I do wish I could see you somewhere though. Maybe we'll get lucky and the two schools will decide to go co-ed before the end of the semester! Ha! Dream on!*

Yours,
Rob

P.S. Like my artwork? It's not as good as yours, but we're not all as arty as you are. (This is a compliment!)

Lisa McGreevy read the letter through three times before carefully folding it back into the blue square envelope. There was nobody on earth like her pen pal, Rob Williams! And now that he'd sent her a piece of his green plaid shirt, the quilt she was making with her three suitemates was bound to be truly sensational.

"It's come!" she cried, taking the stairs three at a time, then bursting into the suite she shared with three other freshmen at Alma Stephens School for Girls. "Rob sent a piece of his shirt! I've got my pen pal patch for the quilt!"

Lisa's roommate and best friend, Shanon Davis, was sitting bare-legged on the floor of the sitting room, scribbling in a leather-bound book. Sunlight spilled in through the open window, highlighting the gold in her pale brown hair. Making the quilt was Shanon's idea. She thought it would be a fun project for them all to work on together—and she was right!

"So Rob finally came through with a scrap of his clothing?" Shanon greeted Lisa, looking up from her journal. "Let's see."

Lisa ceremoniously handed over the green plaid patch.

"It's from his favorite shirt," she sighed. "I remember he wore it last fall at that soccer match we were invited to at Ardsley," she said, referring to the nearby boys' prep school. "It was probably the second or third time I saw him in my whole life. Up until then, we'd only met at the Halloween Mixer and written letters to each other."

Shanon smiled and gave the material back to Lisa. All four of the suitemates were writing to boy pen pals. It was one of the few opportunities for co-ed contact at the all-girl boarding school.

"It's a great piece of fabric," Shanon said enthusiastically. "It'll look excellent on the quilt."

Lisa plopped down on the pink loveseat. "I want to sew it in a really special spot," she said. "Rob's contribution to the quilt should stand out—just like he does!" Lisa glanced at the photograph on the wall. The four girls in the suite had posed with their pen pals. Of the boys they wrote to, Lisa thought Rob was the cutest. He was tall with curly dark hair and a muscular body. Shanon's pen pal Mars was short, Amy's pen pal John was too thin in Lisa's estimation, and Palmer's pen pal Sam O'Leary, though definitely cute, wasn't half as mysterious-looking as Rob—even if he *was* a rock musician.

"Where's the quilt?" Lisa demanded. "I want to sew Rob's patch on right away."

"Palmer and Amy are working on it in their room," Shanon answered. She got up and looked out the window. "This weather is great. It makes me want to go outside. I'd better stop loafing, though, and go study."

"You loaf?" Lisa scoffed. "Give me a break! You don't know the meaning of the word. I, however, am behind in just

3

about everything—especially history. I just haven't got the memory for historical dates!"

"Oh, really?" Shanon giggled. "I bet you remember the date Rob gave you his Ardsley class pin!"

"I'll never forget *that*," Lisa admitted, swooping her dark hair up into a ponytail. "It was the most historic date in my whole history."

The door to Amy and Palmer's room suddenly swung open, and the other two roommates walked into the sitting room. Foxes of the Third Dimension was what they actually called themselves. It was a nickname the girls had thought up when they'd first started rooming together in Suite 3-D of Fox Hall.

"Have you guys been working on the quilt all this time?" asked Shanon.

"You bet," replied Amy. The half-finished crazy quilt was swung over one of her shoulders. Amy Ho, who was Chinese-American, was pretty and athletic-looking. She wore her jet-black hair in a slightly punky, spiked style and was almost always dressed in black.

"I'm *so* glad you thought up this quilt project for us, Shanon!" said tall, blonde Palmer Durand, ambling over to the pink loveseat. "I'd never even sewn a button on at home. And now here I am, helping to make a quilt!"

"As long as one of us threads the needle for you," Lisa quipped playfully. The other girls giggled. Palmer's avid interest in the quilt seemed so out of character. At the beginning of the school year, the pretty junior debutante had kept to herself, spending most of her free time ordering clothes from catalogues. But lately Palmer seemed much more eager to be part of the group.

"I'm glad you're having fun with it, Palmer," said Shanon.

"Of course," she added, "this quilt isn't exactly like the ones my mom and grandmother make at our house."

"No," said Lisa with a grin. "Ours is a true original. It's beginning to look more like a map of the world than a coverlet."

Amy laid the quilt out on the floor. "I love that big lavender piece on the right!" she said.

"It came from my sister Doreen's old skirt," said Shanon.

"And this lacy peach-colored piece from Palmer's party dress looks great, too," Amy chimed in. "I hate to say this, but I've actually been thinking about sacrificing a piece of black leather from my old vest."

"Hey!" Lisa said, hunkering down on the floor. "I never saw that piece before! Who put it in?" She pointed accusingly to a blue triangle in the center of the quilt.

"I did," said Amy. "It's the piece John sent me from his denim shirt."

"That's not fair," Lisa protested. "You put it right in the middle! That's where I was going to put Rob's piece!"

"Sorry," said Amy, "I didn't know. Anyway, I think the blue piece looks good there."

"I thought the idea was for us to design the quilt together," Lisa went on, producing the patch she'd gotten from Rob. "How come you and Palmer took the quilt into your room anyway?"

"Because I ran out of thread," Amy explained, "and then Palmer couldn't wait to add on the patch that Sam O'Leary sent—"

"Isn't it gorgeous!" Palmer chimed in. "It's real silk! I think it must have come from one of Sam's costumes. It's probably from a shirt he wears when he plays with The Fantasy!"

5

"That's not the point," Lisa insisted, "I thought the whole idea of this quilt project was that when we worked on it, we worked on it together. Now Amy's gone and put her pen pal's patch in the best spot without even asking anybody!"

"You mean without asking *you?*" Amy challenged.

Shanon got up. She hated any kind of conflict and was the group's unofficial peacemaker. "It's such a beautiful day," she said. "Too beautiful for an argument, don't you think?"

Lisa looked at Amy, and Amy stared back at Lisa.

"Shanon's right," Lisa quickly admitted. "It's a ridiculous thing to argue about anyway. Sorry, Amy."

"No problem," Amy said good-naturedly.

Lisa sighed. She smoothed the green plaid fabric. "It's just that—well, this is not just a piece of fabric," she explained. "It's something of Rob's I'll always have. It's symbolic! I wonder what he'd think if he knew what I'm really using it for?" she added with a giggle.

Amy laughed. "I told John that Palmer and I were redecorating our room and I needed a piece of his old blue shirt so we could find a bedspread that color!"

"I told Rob I wanted a piece of his shirt to analyze the cotton for chemistry!" Lisa announced.

"Chemistry!" squealed Palmer. "You don't even take chemistry!"

Lisa laughed. "So what? *Rob* doesn't know that. Anyway, I certainly couldn't tell him what it was really for. Not after we all agreed to keep the Fox quilt a secret."

"Absolutely," said Shanon. "We don't want to show it to anybody until it's finished." And picking up Lisa's green plaid patch, she suggested, "Why don't you put Rob's piece over here on the left—in the place of the heart?"

"The what?" said Lisa.

"The heart," said Shanon. "That's on the upper left side of our bodies. If you sew Rob's patch on the upper left side of the quilt, it'll be the heart of the quilt."

"What an exceptional idea!" Lisa exclaimed. "I love it."

Shanon got up. "See you later, gang. I have to go apply myself to something literary."

"Are you going to read that Robert Frost poem for Mr. Griffith's English class?" Palmer asked anxiously. "I could use some help interpreting it."

"Sorry," Shanon said. "I've got to tackle my French paper first."

Palmer groaned and fluffed up her hair. "French—I haven't even started my paper yet. Miss Grayson's going to kill me!"

"And after I finish French," Shanon said, "I've got to work on some sketches for Gina Hawkins."

"Sketches for what?" Lisa asked.

"Haven't you heard?" Shanon said. "Gina's written a play. She's calling it *Everypeople*."

"*Everypeople*?" said Palmer. "What a weird title."

"It's a takeoff on the fifteenth-century morality play *Everyman*," Shanon explained.

"Well, whatever it is, it sounds heavy," Palmer decided.

Shanon sat down again. "The original play was *very* heavy," she agreed. "The main character, a person called Everyman, had to go on a journey with Death!"

"Yuk!" said Lisa. "How morbid! Is Gina's play going to be like that?"

"I don't think so," said Shanon. "In Gina's play there are a couple of characters called Everyman and Everywoman who go on a journey, but they don't die in the end. They go to the center of the earth and end up happy. But the main

7

difference is that Gina's play is a rock musical."

"Wow!" cried Amy. She ran to grab her guitar. "A rock musical? This is just what I've been waiting for!"

"You ought to try out," said Shanon. "You all should."

Palmer rolled her eyes. "Not me. I can think of nothing more boring than another one of those all-girl productions. Hey, who's going to play Everyman? Are they going to make some poor girl put on a fake mustache?"

Shanon laughed. "No, that would be awful. There are going to be *boys* in this play, from what Gina told me."

Lisa's big brown eyes got wider. "Boys? What boys?"

Shanon shrugged. "Ardies, I guess. Gina's going to audition them. She's even got some boy lined up as music director."

"This is fantastic!" Lisa cried. She looked at Amy and Palmer. "Don't you see?"

"See what?" said Amy.

"There are going to be Ardies in the play," Lisa said. "That means Rob! Or John or Mars."

"What about Sam?" said Palmer. " He's a natural for a rock 'n' roll play. He's even got his own band!"

"True," said Amy, "but Sam doesn't go to Ardsley."

"Who cares about that?" huffed Palmer. "If Sam O'Leary auditions for the lead in a rock musical, he's bound to get it."

"Maybe, maybe not," said Lisa. "Rob likes acting, too. And he's definitely the leading-man type."

"Is there going to be a leading man?" Amy asked.

"Of course," said Shanon. "It's Everyman. And Gina says there's a leading girl's part, too—Everywoman. I guess she's Everyman's girlfriend."

"Wow!" said Amy. "This is great!" She strummed a loud

chord on her guitar. "This could be the break I'm looking for! I'll be in this play and be discovered!"

"You're not the only one who's going to try out." Lisa laughed. "And I'm going to write Rob about the boy's part right away."

"I might as well write to John," said Amy, "though I don't really think he's the actor type."

"Well, I'm definitely going to tell Sam," said Palmer. "Not only that, I'm going to try out for a part myself! Everyone's always telling me I look like a movie star."

Lisa giggled. "Are you sure it won't be too 'boring' for you?" she said slyly.

"Oh, I'll manage," said Palmer dreamily. "Just imagine—if Sam and I both get parts in the play, we'll be able to spend hours together!"

"Yes," Lisa sighed, "that's what I'm thinking about, too." She turned to Shanon. "What about you? Are you going to try out? Maybe Mars could get a part, too."

"I think I'll just stick with the costumes," Shanon said, flushing. "I can't see myself in front of an audience. I'm not much of an actress, and I can't sing a note. As for Mars, I'll certainly tell him about the auditions. As soon as I finish my French," she added, marching determinedly into her room.

"I'm going to stay out here and write to Rob," said Lisa, grabbing a pen and paper from the desk. "When are the auditions going to be?" she called after Shanon.

"Soon," Shanon replied from the other room. "Gina's going to announce it."

Lisa snuggled back on the loveseat. Amy and Palmer sat down on either side of her.

"Pretty exciting, huh?" said Amy. "Can we have some paper?"

Lisa tore two sheets from her tablet while Palmer got up to get more pens.

"I just hope we *all* get parts in the play," Lisa said uneasily. "Remember what happened when Shanon and I were both running for dorm rep?"

Palmer rolled her blue eyes. "How could we forget? I just hope we don't get all competitive about this."

"We won't," said Amy, grabbing a pen from her. "Anyway, we're not necessarily going to be trying out for the same parts. I bet there are loads of girls' parts in Gina's play."

"And loads of girls auditioning," said Palmer.

"Everyman and Everywoman, huh?" Amy chuckled. "Definitely rad! Whatever happens . . . it should be very interesting."

CHAPTER TWO

———— ✒ ————

Dear Rob,

   I really appreciate your sacrificing your green plaid shirt. It was perfect for my chemistry experiment. But on to other news! An Alma girl named Gina Hawkins is putting on her own play here! And Ardies are invited to audition! How would you like to try out? I am definitely going to. The play is called Everypeople. *I'm sure you could beat out most of the competition for the boys' roles. So I hope you try out. If we both got parts, we could see each other in rehearsal. I'm really excited about this. Write soon.*

                                                   Lisa

Dear Sam,

   I thought you might like to know that there is a play being put on at our school. I don't know too many details yet, but it's definitely a rock and roll musical and has a leading boy part that you would be perfect for. So why don't you try out? I'm going to. Then we could be in it together. What's new with *The Fantasy?* And how is your job at Suzy's Shoe Emporium? Write soon.

Palmer

Dear John,

The big news around here is Gina Hawkins's new play, Everypeople. *I'm trying out. For my audition, I think I'll sing the first song we collaborated on in our letters—"Cabin Fever." How about trying out yourself? I know you don't like to sing, but maybe you are a good actor. How's your poetry writing? I hope it's going well. I am still listening to a lot of music, mostly The Grateful Dead, Paul Simon, Tracy Chapman, Michael Jackson, and The Beatles. Advanced math is still difficult. I am beginning to wish I hadn't been so advanced and gotten into the class. So long for now.*

Amy

Dear Mars,

I am doing the costumes for the school play here. Have you ever been in a play? I was, once. It was a Thanksgiving play in my old grammar school and I was a Pilgrim. I only had one line to say, but I forgot it the second I stepped onto the stage! That was the end of my acting career. How about you? Maybe you'd like to audition for this. Maybe there's a role for a comedian. To me you have always had a great sense of humor. Coming up with ideas for the costumes for Gina's play is truly challenging. She wants them to look old-fashioned yet also be modern. She wants them to be fashionable and at the same time comfortable. She wants

them to all look alike but still be different. Got any ideas?
Write soon.

Sincerely,
Shanon

earDay anonShay,

eckChay itay outay!—igpay atinlay! NO, Iay illway ot-
nay ytray outay orfay Everypeopleay! Ifay ethay amenay
ofay ethay ayplay asway Everypigay, aybemay Iay ouldway
ytray outay. Iay ovelay igpays. yMay avoritefay etpay asway
aay igpay amednay ilburWay.

oveLay,
arsMay artinezMay

P.S. I will not tax your mind further with my favorite code.
As for the costumes, the obvious solution is birthday suits—
both modern and primitive, fashionable yet comfortable.
But this is probably against the dress code and your headmistress, Miss Pryn, would have you suspended, so you'd
better keep thinking. By the way, what was your favorite pet
when you were little? I hope your family had more imagi-
nation than mine did—Wilbur is not a very original name
for a pig.

Dear Amy,

Enclosed is a poem I wrote, hot off the presses—or in this
case, my typewriter. I am sending some of my work down
to the Brighton Library. They are sponsoring a poetry
reading for young writers, and I hope to be included in it.
Please give me your honest opinion about this one. I trust
your taste.

13

Negative
Zero hour
Playing baseball
In the cloudy field of life
I wave my cap at the sun
Its rays don't bother me
But I like moonlight
Masculine/Feminine

Yours truly,
John

P.S. *I'm going to try out for the play, too, but against my better judgment as I will probably embarrass myself. Mars is definitely not trying out, even though Shanon asked him to. That guy is really something! Remember when he was into parrots? Well, his latest thing is pigs! And since he can't have a real one at school, he's been going all over the campus in a pig mask. Last week he came to the library like that. Even for an Ardie, he is truly outrageous.*

Dear Palmer,
It was great hearing from you. The play at Alma Stephens sounds interesting. Things are going great for The Fantasy. In fact, we have been invited to make a special guest appearance at a shopping mall in Newton, Mass. It is the opening of the mall, and my mom is going to drive the whole band there in a van. Is there any way you could come and see us perform? As I said, my mom will be driving.

Yours truly,
Sam O'Leary

Dear Lisa,
I just got your letter, but I'd already heard about the

14

audition. The guy from Ardsley who is going to be the musical director mentioned it to me. What a great idea for a play—making something modern out of something so old. I hear all the characters are going to be punked-out rockers. I love acting! My singing voice is not the greatest, but I am definitely going to do my best to get a speaking part. And knowing you'll be in the play (because I'm sure if you audition, you'll get a part—probably the lead) is a great motivator. The track coach is running me into the ground these days, but my time is improving.

Your fellow thespian,
Rob

CHAPTER THREE

---◆---

CASTING NOTICE

Everypeople, a two-act rock musical written and directed by Gina Hawkins (Music Director, Bob Brown of Ardsley Academy), announces auditions for the following roles:

Girls' Roles:
EVERYWOMAN—leading lady: requires a rock singing voice
SOUL—narrator of the story: must sing and speak well
HOME—must be a good actress, with sweet folk-singing voice
Chorus Parts: ACCOMPLISHMENTS, PRIDE, HEART, and BEAUTY

Boys' Roles:
EVERYMAN—leading man: this role has some singing but also requires a strong actor
Chorus Parts: RICHES, GOOD TIMES, COURAGE, and PEACE
This is an open call. Boys will be selected from students of Ardsley Academy.
For further information, contact Gina Hawkins, director, or Kate Majors, stage manager. Ardsley students may contact Bob Brown.

"It's not fair!" complained Palmer. "Why can't boys from Brighton High audition?"

Gina Hawkins looked thoughtful. She was a lovely black girl with light brown skin, golden eyes, and wavy black hair. A fourth-former, she was a year older than the Foxes.

"I suppose it's school tradition to only do things with Ardsley since that's a private school just like Alma," Gina told Palmer. "I guess it's always been that way around here."

"Well, that still doesn't make it fair!" Palmer huffed.

"I agree," said Gina. "But I'm just the writer and director of *Everypeople*. I don't set school policy."

"I've got a friend who goes to Brighton, and he'd be great for your play," Palmer went on hotly. "Have you ever heard of Sam and The Fantasy?"

"They're a local group," Gina replied. "I like their sound a lot."

"Well, Sam O'Leary can't even try out for your play," Palmer said, "because of this stupid policy."

"When are the boys' auditions taking place?" Lisa interrupted. She sympathized with Palmer, but at the moment she was thinking only of Rob.

"Next Saturday at Ardsley," Gina replied, "right after we have the girls' auditions over here."

"Too bad the boys and girls can't audition together," Brenda Smith said, fluffing her frizzy blonde hair. "My boyfriend isn't trying out, but I'd like to see some of the other competition, especially for Everyman."

Dawn Hubbard giggled. "What I want to know is how are you going to tell whether he's a *strong* actor? Will you make all the boys wear muscle shirts?"

The group broke out into giggles.

Gina smiled and got up from the table. "I wasn't actually thinking about their physiques," she said. "I'm looking for a strong *personality*!"

"Good thing," said Muffin Talbot. "There are a lot of puny boys at Ardsley."

"Not all of them," Lisa announced, pushing her way closer to Gina.

"I have to go to study hall now," Gina said over the other girls' laughter. "This play is taking up so much of my time, I've been letting my schoolwork slide." As she headed down the corridor, Lisa ran after her.

"Gina, can I talk to you for a minute?" Lisa asked breathlessly.

"Sure," Gina said, barely slowing down.

Lisa felt suddenly nervous. It wasn't as if Gina Hawkins was a famous writer or director, but being in the play with Rob was so important to her.

"What's on your mind?" Gina prompted.

"Well," Lisa began, "I have this boy . . . I mean friend . . . actually, he's my pen pal."

Gina gave her an understanding smile. "And he's trying out for the play, is that it?"

"Yes," said Lisa. "He has a very strong personality! and strong muscles, too! You'll recognize him right away. His name is Rob Williams."

Gina smiled. "I'll remember that." She glanced at the clock. "But now I've really got to—"

"Just a minute," pressed Lisa. "What kinds of things will you be looking for in the auditions? Or isn't it fair for me to ask you that?"

"No, it's okay to ask," Gina replied. "I'm just looking for

people who can relax and be themselves on stage. Of course they've got to be able to sing and act, too."

Lisa looked bewildered. "That's all? So I should just tell Rob to be himself?"

"That would be my advice," Gina answered.

"And what about Everywoman?" Lisa prodded. "What advice would you give for somebody trying to be her?"

Gina's golden eyes looked thoughtful again. "That's a very special role. Even more important than the boy's lead. All I can say is that Everywoman is an original. Someone who is strong and very confident."

"Thanks, Gina," Lisa said as the older girl walked away. Lisa stood in one spot for a moment, wondering if she was really an original. She had certainly always been confident.

"What did she say?" Palmer asked, coming up behind her.

"She told me to be myself at the auditions," Lisa said blithely. "That should be easy enough."

Amy fell in with them and the three suitemates walked to the dining room. "She also said to be confident," Lisa added as they joined the lunch line.

"Well, that should be no problem for you," said Amy. "I think you'd be great for the lead."

Lisa smiled. "Really?"

"Sure," said Amy, grabbing a salad. "Personally, I'd rather be Soul. I hear she has the most singing because she's the narrator."

Lisa helped herself to a ham and cheese sandwich and a carton of milk, while Mrs. Butter, the school cook, served a hot lunch to Palmer.

"Too bad the guys won't be coming over here to audition," Amy said. "I'd love to see John again."

"Yes, it's a bummer," said Lisa, grabbing some pie.

Palmer plunked her plate down onto her tray. "At least Rob and John *can* audition," she griped. "This policy of never including the public schools in our activities is terrible."

Lisa shrugged. "They're townies."

"So what? Shanon's a townie, too," Palmer pointed out as the girls made their way toward their favorite center table. "She grew up in Brighton, too. You mean, if she hadn't gotten into Alma Stephens, we wouldn't be allowed to associate with her?"

"If Shanon hadn't gotten into Alma, we wouldn't have met her in the first place," Amy argued.

"That's not the point," Palmer protested. "I can't believe the two of you are talking like that!" She sat down angrily.

"Chill out," said Lisa, taking her own seat. "I think it's a dumb rule, too, and so does Amy I'm sure. But you can't change the system."

"Why not?" Palmer pouted. "Isn't that what the Student Council is for?"

Amy munched a stick of celery. "Sure. But you aren't on the Student Council."

Just then Shanon dashed into the dining hall and waved at them from the food line. Minutes later she joined them with her lunch tray.

"You'll never believe what I just saw!" Shanon greeted them breathlessly. "It was incredible!"

"What was?" Lisa asked, taking a bite of her sandwich.

"Something . . ." Shanon glanced around and took a seat, "personal." She lowered her voice. "Something romantic!"

Palmer wrinkled her nose. "Romantic? In this place? How?"

20

Shanon's hazel eyes twinkled. "Just because there are no boy students here, doesn't mean that romantic things can't happen," she whispered.

"Then it must be about Miss Grayson and Mr. Griffith!" Amy squealed, leaning in. Miss Grayson was the girls' dorm adviser as well as their French teacher. And Mr. Griffith taught them English. Both of the teachers were young and very attractive.

"Did you see something?" Lisa said. "Tell us!"

"Well," Shanon confided, with a giggle, "you know how Maggie and Dan are always together." She giggled again, automatically lowering her voice when she said their first names. "They—"

"Those two are in love!" Lisa broke in.

"We *think* they're in love," said Amy. "There's never been any proof of that."

"There is now!" Shanon exclaimed. "I was on my way to the library after French class because I had to do some more research on—"

"Get to the point," Palmer urged impatiently.

"The point," Shanon said, "is that I just saw Miss Grayson and Mr. Griffith near the back entrance of Booth Hall, and they . . ."

"What?" squeaked Lisa.

Shanon took a deep breath. "They were kissing!"

"Oh, my gosh," gasped Palmer.

"We were right all along," Amy said. "They *are* in love! This makes it definite!"

"Wow!" said Lisa. "What kind of kiss was it?"

Shanon fiddled with a side curl. "Actually, it was a small kiss. A quick one also. But," she added, "it definitely looked significant."

Lisa sighed. "Significant, huh? That *is* romantic. Once Rob almost kissed me."

"We know," teased Amy. "We've heard about it a hundred times. It was the morning of the Strawberry Breakfast."

"Yes," Lisa sighed. "The morning he gave me his pin."

"Good grief!" said Shanon, suddenly noticing the time. "We've got three minutes to get to history."

As the girls headed toward the door, Lisa told Shanon about her conversation with Gina Hawkins, and then asked, "Have you shown her your costume sketches?"

"Yes," Shanon replied. "But Gina doesn't think they're quite right, so I've got to do some more. At least we've definitely decided on the material."

"What kind of material will you be using?" Lisa asked curiously.

Shanon smiled. "Patchwork!"

"Patchwork!" exclaimed Amy. "As in the Fox quilt?"

"Don't worry," said Shanon, "I didn't tell her anything about that. But I think the color and design can be really interesting if I piece the material together. I won't use a lot of little pieces like in the quilt, but big ones with lots of prints and bright colors."

"You're sewing the costumes, too?" Palmer asked in amazement.

"I think it'll be fun," Shanon said enthusiastically. "Dawn Hubbard is lending me her sewing machine so I can work in the suite."

Lisa shook her dark head. "Leave it to my roommate! It's not enough that you're on the Student Council and write for *The Ledger*—now you're going to make all the costumes for *Everypeople*."

"Not all of them," Shanon corrected her. "Just the ones

22

for the girls. Some Ardie is working with Gina and Bob Brown on the boys' costumes."

"Wow!" said Amy. "A boy who sews!"

"Why not?" quipped Lisa. "You can do carpentry."

Having left the dining hall and taken a shortcut across the quad, the girls arrived at the History and Science building just as the big clock on the tower was chiming. They hurried inside and raced down the hall to their class.

Mr. Seganish cleared his throat as they entered. As usual, they were the last four to enter the classroom. "Well, well," the teacher teased, "look who's here."

"We're not really late," Shanon volunteered politely. "The clock is still chiming."

"Take your seats then," instructed the teacher, "and let's see how much you know about the Watergate affair."

Lisa gulped. "The what?" she whispered to Amy.

"It was a big government scandal," Amy whispered back.

Shanon took a seat near the back of the room, and Palmer followed her.

"There was something important I wanted to ask you," Palmer whispered.

"I—"

Mr. Seganish rapped his pencil and glanced pointedly at the back of the room. Palmer lowered her eyes and stopped talking. Then she scribbled something in her notebook, tore out the page, and passed it over to Shanon.

I have a problem that has to do with Sam. I hope you can help me.

CHAPTER FOUR

———————◆———————

Dear Sam,

Bad news! I just found out that the only boys who can audition for our play at Alma are boys that go to Ardsley Academy! By now you have probably found that out, too. I think it is rotten, and this is what I did. My suitemate Shanon is on the Alma Student Council, and she is really nice. Not only that, but she grew up in the town of Brighton and her sister Doreen went to your school. So I asked Shanon to bring this up at the next meeting of the Student Council. And guess what? The Council thought it was weird that boys from Brighton High couldn't try out for the play also.

Unfortunately, it took them two whole meetings to write a letter to our headmistress, Miss Pryn, about it. Then she wrote back and said that asking Brighton to participate in the theater project would mean a whole change in policy because Alma only does things with Ardsley. And then she said that she would get back to the Student Council with her answer on this, but first she'd have to discuss it with the Board! This stinks because by the time that happens, the auditions for Everypeople *will be over.*

I really am sorry. To be completely honest, before I knew you, I used to be kind of snobby about public schools myself. But now I see how dumb that is and how dumb Alma's policy is if it keeps people like you and me from seeing each other.

Anyway, your gig at the shopping mall sounds much more exciting than Gina's play. Now that you can't audition, I am not going to either. It sounds like a very intellectual play, and I am not exactly the intellectual type. I can hardly wait to come hear you sing at the Newton mall.

> Yours truly,
> Palmer

Dear John,

I'm so glad you are going to audition for Everypeople. Trying out for the poetry reading at the Brighton Library also sounds exciting. I hope you get a chance to be in it. I liked your latest poem a lot.

I showed your letter to Shanon, and she thought the part about Mars and the pig mask was very funny. Did you know he wrote his last letter to her in Pig Latin? Let me know how you do in your tryout for the play, and I will let you know how I do in mine.

> Good luck,
> Amy

earDay arsMay,

Iay owknay igpay atinlay ootay. Iay alsoay ikelay igspay. utBay ymay avoritefay etpay atay omehay asway aay oatgay.

The goat's name was Beasle, and he ate everything. My parents could not control him. Not only that, he was always

25

butting us. But everyone liked him anyway and thought he was funny—until he got into my dad's garage and gobbled up a bunch of expensive tires. Then my dad said, "Beasle must go!" So we sold him to a farmer, and the farmer came to take him away in a pickup truck. The whole back of the truck was full of cabbage heads. The farmer tied Beasle's rope to the inside wall of the truck. It was sad. Beasle's head was almost against the wall. But by the time the farmer took off, we could see that Beasle was already free! He had chewed his rope off. Not only that, he was eating the cabbages. They probably tasted much better than tires! By the way, even though Wilbur was the pig in Charlotte's Web, I still think it's a very cute name.

I don't blame you for not wanting to be in the play. I have no desire to be in it either. As you may have noticed, I'm really more of a behind-the-scenes type. The costumes are going okay. Lately I have been doing a lot of sewing (some of which I can't talk about!). Though your suggestion about the birthday suits is really funny, I agree with you that Miss Pryn would probably not be amused. Speaking of costumes, I hear you are wearing a pig outfit in the library. When do you find time to study?

> Oinkay-oinkay,
> anonShay

P.S. If the play were called Everypig, would you try out then?
P.P.S. My dad once told me that during the war, one code that the enemy could never break was Pig Latin!

Dear Rob,

I have some hot tips for you! At the audition, just be yourself! That's what Gina Hawkins told me. She is also *looking for the strong type, so I suggest you wear your green muscle shirt. Hope you don't mind the advice, but I have a feeling you are going to get the lead in this play. And I'm going all out for the girl's lead. In fact, I am doing a lot of research on medieval times. I am going to try very hard to be myself and confident, but at the same time medieval. Not only that, every time I see Gina Hawkins, she smiles at me, so I think she wants me in her play.*

Good luck! And see you on "the boards"!

Lisa

CHAPTER FIVE

—◆—

"How do I look?" asked Lisa, twirling around like a model. She was wearing an old-fashioned blue and white peasant dress and a round medieval-looking hat.

Palmer peered over the top of her magazine. "Like Snow White with a doughnut on her head," she said flatly.

"That's not true!" Lisa said, rushing to the mirror. She adjusted the string bodice on the dress and placed her hat at a sharper angle. "I look like someone right out of the Middle Ages! This costume I borrowed from Dawn is just like one of the pictures in Shanon's costume book! As a matter of fact, I think I look exactly like Everywoman! I just hope Gina thinks so, too."

Amy came out of her room with her guitar and a bunch of guitar strings. "Wow, look at you," she said, taking in Lisa's outfit. "You look just like a jester."

"I'm not supposed to be a jester," Lisa groaned. "I'm supposed to be Everywoman!"

Amy shrugged. "Oh, right. . . . I guess I'm just going to go this way," she said, smoothing her black spandex jogging suit over her hips.

"What song are you singing?" Lisa asked, fiddling with her hat some more.

" 'Cabin Fever,' " Amy replied. "What are you singing?"

"A Beatles song," said Lisa " 'Let It Be' . . . if I can remember the words." She put on some lipstick, then added blush and eyeliner. "Do you think they had makeup in the Middle Ages? Even if they didn't, I'm wearing some," she said decisively. "It'll make me look better onstage."

"Good idea," Amy agreed, "especially if they put on the stage lights."

Palmer let out a loud sigh and tossed down her magazine. "Aren't you two ever going to talk about anything besides this dumb play?" she said.

"But the audition's this morning!" said Lisa. "And it's very important to us."

"But it's *not* at all important to me," Palmer insisted.

"You could still change your mind and try out," Amy said gently.

"Why should I," challenged Palmer, "if Sam can't?"

Amy shrugged. "Because it might be an interesting experience."

"I never was very interested in drama anyway," Palmer admitted. "Besides, I can't sing *or* act."

"Well, I can sing *and* act!" Lisa declared.

Palmer rolled her eyes. "And no one can say you're not confident!"

Lisa giggled. "That's the idea. I'm confident, and I'm going to be myself, and I'm going to convince everybody at the audition that I am perfect for Everywoman!" She put on another layer of lipstick and sprayed on some perfume.

"I'm glad one of us feels confident," said Amy, replacing

a broken E string on her guitar. "We're not even there yet and already my knees are knocking."

Palmer got up dramatically and headed for her bedroom.

"Hey, I'm sorry," said Amy. "I was talking about the audition again. Don't leave the room. We're going."

"That's okay," Palmer called back. "I'd better get started on that French paper. Otherwise, I'll never get to see Sam O'Leary."

"How come?" said Lisa, wandering over to the bedroom.

Palmer rolled her eyes. "Miss Grayson has to give me permission to go to the shopping mall concert. And she'll never let me have a pass if she thinks I'm behind in my studies. She's the one I'm doing the French paper for."

"Sounds like you'd better get to work," Lisa said sympathetically before walking back into the sitting room. "Ready?" she asked Amy.

Amy took a deep breath. "Ready as I'll ever be. I've practiced my audition piece a thousand times. Now it's all in the hands of Fate."

Lisa giggled. "And Gina Hawkins." Giving herself a last-minute check in the mirror, she felt her heart begin to pound. "I just hope I get my part," she said nervously.

"I hope we both do," said Amy, running her hands through her hair.

"Hey, wait," said Lisa. She gave Amy a serious look. "I just wanted to check on something."

"What?" said Amy, picking up her guitar case.

Lisa laughed uncomfortably. "We did agree that we're not trying out for the same part, right?"

"I guess so," said Amy. "I want to be Soul."

"Great," Lisa said. "Because if you tried out for Everywoman, it would really lessen my chances. You sing so much better than I do!"

"Don't put yourself down," said Amy. "You're a good actress. Anyway, we want different roles, so we're not competing."

"Okay," said Lisa, relieved. She grabbed Amy's hand and squeezed it. "Good luck!" she said.

Amy squeezed her hand back. "Good luck yourself!"

Gina was holding the auditions in the new school theater. Lisa peeked in at the stage from the lobby. It looked enormous! Then she glanced around at the other would-be actors gathered outside. They were all wearing their regular clothes. She began to feel kind of silly. She felt even sillier when Gina came up to her and said, "Hey, Lisa, how come you're dressed like that?"

"I—I thought. . . ." As Lisa fumbled for an explanation, the peasant dress and doughnut hat suddenly felt ridiculous.

"It's okay," said Gina, "I understand. You're probably trying to get into character. But when you see the whole script, you'll understand that *Everypeople* is quite modern. In fact, Shanon and I have finally settled on the costumes, and they're going to look something like running suits."

"Running suits?" said Lisa. She looked at Amy. "Like the kind Amy's wearing?"

"Sort of," Gina chuckled. "Anyway, you look beautiful in that dress. Grab a side from Kate and take a look at the scene. Did you bring any sheet music for your song?"

Lisa gulped. "Sheet music? I didn't know somebody would be here to play the piano, and I don't play the guitar like Amy does."

"That's okay," said Gina. "You can sing your song a capella."

Sweat broke out on Lisa's forehead. "Aca what . . . ?"

"Without any accompaniment," Gina explained. She left Lisa standing there, breathing nervously.

"Hey, have you seen the side we're going to be reading?" asked Amy, coming up to her.

"Side?" Lisa echoed.

"The audition scene," said Amy. She gave Lisa a sheet. "I got one for you from Kate."

Lisa looked at the typewritten scene eagerly. "Great," she murmured. "It's a scene for Everywoman. That means Gina has me in mind for the role."

"Not exactly," said Amy. "That's the scene she gave everybody."

Lisa looked around at the group of girls in the lobby. They were all studying the identical scene. "That's dumb," she said. "How is she going to know what parts people are good for, if she has everybody reading the same lines?"

"Beats me," said Amy. "Anyway, I'm going to tell her that I'm interested in the part of Soul."

"Good idea," said Lisa. "And I'll tell her I want to be Everywoman."

Lisa found a chair and sat down to study the scene. The writing was very poetic. It was a farewell scene between Everywoman and Everyman. Lisa imagined herself and Rob doing it. It would be a dream come true if they both got the leads.

Lisa looked up as Gina came out of the theater again. "Ready everybody?" the director began in a friendly voice. "Just by way of explanation, our stage manager, Kate Majors, will be reading the part of Everyman with you today.

32

Mr. Griffith, who's our faculty adviser from the English department, will also be watching you audition. And Bob Brown, the music director from Ardsley, will naturally be sitting in, too."

"Wow," Lisa whispered, "that's a lot of people."

"You're not kidding," Amy said quietly. "But just think how many people will be in the audience when the play actually goes on."

"Okay—let's get started," said Gina. "Who wants to go first?"

Amy shot up out of her chair. "Might as well get it over," she said with a grin. She turned and waved to Lisa. "Here goes. . . ."

While Amy auditioned in the theater, Lisa sat out in the lobby and looked over her lines. Through the door she could hear Amy singing.

"She sounds great," said Muffin Talbot, at Lisa's elbow.

"Amy has a terrific voice, all right," Brenda Smith agreed. "It'll be hard to beat her out for the lead."

Lisa looked up. "Oh, she's not trying out for that," she said. "Amy wants to play Soul."

"Rats!" Brenda muttered. "That's the part *I* wanted."

There was a moment's silence in the lobby. Then the door to the theater swung open, and Amy came out looking relieved and happy.

"How did it go?" Lisa said, jumping up.

"I think I did okay," said Amy.

"You sounded wonderful," Brenda chimed in just as Kate Majors stuck her head out the door.

"Next!"

"I'll go," Lisa volunteered bravely.

As soon as she entered the theater, Lisa spotted Gina

sitting in the front row of seats next to a chubby red-haired boy. Mr. Griffith was directly behind them in the fifth row.

"Hello, Miss McGreevy," Mr. Griffith said as Lisa passed. The young English teacher was wearing a sea-green tie that brought out the color of his eyes.

"Hi, Mr. Griffith," she gulped. "Hi, Gina."

Gina pointed to the boy beside her. "This is Bob Brown."

Lisa smiled and nodded.

"Don't be nervous," Gina said as Kate Majors hopped onto the stage. "Just read the scene with Kate. Then we'll hear your song."

"Okay," said Lisa. Her heart pounded loudly as she climbed the stairs of the huge new stage and stood opposite Kate. It was hard to think of the mousy-looking stage manager as Everyman, so Lisa decided to imagine that instead of Kate she was reading the scene with a handsome boy—someone like Rob. Gluing her eyes to the paper, she cleared her throat.

"Okay," said Gina. "You can start now."

Lisa began to read. "Everyman, your soul and mine are one! But we must not journey together. To find the buried treasure at the earth's center, we must search each on our own."

"I know that to be true," Kate Majors read flatly.

Lisa took a breath. "My companions will be Accomplishments, Heart, and Pride. If these friends do not desert me, I will surely find the treasure."

"Farewell," Kate read.

"Farewell," Lisa read. "We will meet again. This I promise."

Gina stood up. "Great reading, Lisa."

34

"Very nice," Mr. Griffith agreed.

"That's all?" Lisa asked.

Gina leaned over and whispered something to Bob Brown. Then she turned back to Lisa. "I'd like to hear your song now."

After Lisa sang "Let It Be" in a clear, sweet soprano, Gina whispered to Bob again. Lisa broke out into a sweat. She hoped their whispering was a good sign.

"Okay," Gina said, "that'll be it. I'd have you read some of the scenes for Beauty, Home, and the other girls' chorus parts, but I'm still working those out."

"That's all right," said Lisa. "Anyway, I'm not trying out for those parts. I want to be Everywoman."

"I'll keep that in mind," said Gina. "Thanks for coming in today."

Lisa scooted out of the theater and found Amy waiting at the door.

"Am I glad that's over!" Lisa exclaimed.

"What happened?" asked Amy. "Didn't it go well?"

"I guess it did," said Lisa, "but I wasn't sure what they wanted me to do. I tried to act confident, but all I felt was scared."

"I was scared, too," Amy admitted.

"But your singing sounded so great through the door," Lisa said. "I could hardly remember the words to 'Let It Be.' "

"You sounded fine from here," Amy assured her.

Kate poked her head out again. "Shhh! Quiet out here!"

As Amy and Lisa guiltily stepped outside, they could hear Kate's authoritative voice calling, "Next!"

"Well, whatever happens," said Amy, "at least we weren't afraid to try out."

"That's right," said Lisa, taking off her doughnut hat. "I think we deserve a treat for that."

Amy grinned and pointed toward Booth Hall. "To the snack bar?"

"To the snack bar!" said Lisa. "For two double choc-shots!"

Shanon knocked on the door to Miss Grayson's cozy little apartment in the basement of Fox Hall.

"Shanon! How are you?" Miss Grayson's curly reddish hair was tied up in a kerchief, and she was wearing shorts and a work shirt. It was obvious she wasn't expecting anyone.

"I'm sorry to disturb you," Shanon said, blushing.

Miss Grayson smiled encouragingly. "Did we have an appointment?"

"No," Shanon replied. "I was just on my way to see Gina about the *Everypeople* play and . . ."

"That's right! You wanted some old clothes for costumes!"

Shanon blushed again. Gina had asked her to collect some secondhand clothing to make the material. But Shanon was also eager to get something of Miss Grayson's for the Fox quilt.

"You're in luck," Miss Grayson said, motioning her into the apartment. "I was just clearing out some things. There's a whole bag of old clothes by the bookcase." She pointed to an overstuffed shopping bag.

Shanon made a beeline for the bag. "This looks great!" she said. "I'm sure we can use some of the material!" She picked up a flower-printed blouse and asked shyly, "How come you're throwing so many clothes away?"

"I find putting things in order can be very therapeutic,"

Miss Grayson replied, brushing a curl back from her face.

"I don't think I understand," Shanon said.

The young teacher chuckled. "Whenever I have something on my mind, I clean out my closets and bookcases," she explained. "I find it quite relaxing. And before I know it, all my thoughts seem to be in order, too."

Shanon smiled. "Oh, I see what you mean. What a good idea!"

"I'm also thinning out my books," the teacher said, wandering over to her book shelf. "Feel free to go through them—"

"I'd love to," Shanon said, eying a carton eagerly.

"—when you get back this evening," Miss Grayson finished. "Right now I have to get ready for an appointment."

"With Mr. Griffith?" Shanon blurted out.

Miss Grayson's face turned bright red.

So did Shanon's. "I'm sorry," she mumbled. "It's none of my business."

"My appointment is in town—with the dentist," Miss Grayson quickly added. "But since you brought him up," she continued in a firm tone, "perhaps you can give Mr. Griffith this for me."

"Sure," said Shanon as the teacher handed her a big brown envelope.

"Thank you," Miss Grayson said crisply. "You'll surely run into him at the theater. I know he was planning to be at the auditions, and I . . . I'm not sure when I'll next see him."

"Okay," Shanon gulped. "Should I give him a message?"

"I'll write one on the envelope," Miss Grayson said quickly. Taking the envelope from Shanon, she hastily scribbled a message and then handed it back again. "Now, if you don't mind . . ." she said.

"Sure . . . yes . . ." Shanon stumbled, "I'm sorry to have taken up your time. And thank you for the clothing."

With the envelope under one arm and the bag of clothes in the other, Shanon scooted out of the apartment. Miss Grayson shut the door quickly behind her.

Something was definitely wrong, Shanon thought as she hurried down the hall. First Miss Grayson had seemed happy. But then as soon as Mr. Griffith's name came up, she'd looked sad and upset—so upset she had practically shoved Shanon out the door. That wasn't at all like Miss Grayson.

Shanon put the shopping bag down near the doorway. She pulled out a flowery blouse to save for the Fox quilt. Then she glanced at the big brown envelope. The words JOB SEARCH were printed on the front. She turned the envelope over. The note Miss Grayson had scribbled was staring right at her.

Shanon shut her eyes, then opened them up again quickly. She knew it was rude to read the note, but she just couldn't help herself. Besides, she reasoned, if the note had been private, Miss Grayson wouldn't have just put it on the outside of the envelope where Shanon could see. And before she could talk herself out of it, Shanon ran her eyes hastily over her teacher's writing:

Dear Dan,
Good luck in making your choices!   M.

Shanon deposited the printed blouse in the suite, then made her way to the theater. All the way there, she thought about Miss Grayson and Mr. Griffith. She hoped nothing was wrong between her two favorite teachers.

CHAPTER SIX

———◆———

"Doesn't this flowered piece from Miss Grayson's blouse look incredible next to Amy's black leather?" Shanon exclaimed. She and Lisa were sitting around the quilt while Palmer carefully sewed the new patch on.

"Ouch!" cried Palmer. "I stuck myself!"

"Never mind," said Lisa. "Your stitches are getting much more even." She pulled a scrap of crimson satin from the shopping bag. "It's a good thing you collected all this material," she said to Shanon. "If I'd cut up any more of my own clothes, I wouldn't have much of a wardrobe."

"Oh, I wouldn't go that far," Shanon said, eying Lisa's beautiful new silk blouse.

Lisa pulled a green piece of velvet out of the bag and said, "At least it's going to good use. This quilt is going to be gorgeous!"

"It is, isn't it?" Shanon replied proudly. "I just hope the *Everypeople* costumes turn out half as well. Of course, I'm not quite sure how patchwork is going to look when it's made into the pants and mini-skirts Gina wants for the play."

"Pants *and* skirts?" said Lisa. "I thought the costumes were going to be like jogging suits."

"They are," Shanon explained. "Sort of. The girls are going to wear these fitted pants—just like running tights—but with a miniskirt on top."

"What about blouses?" Lisa asked.

"Leotards," Shanon replied. "And the boys will be wearing black jeans and hand-painted T-shirts."

"If you ask me," volunteered Palmer, "these costumes are going to look like clown outfits."

Shanon chuckled. "I hope not. Actually, they're supposed to look kind of punky."

"Mail call!" yelled Amy, walking into the suite. She was wearing a short, black jeans skirt with a bright red leotard. "Letters for Lisa and Palmer!"

Palmer jumped up and grabbed a thin, blue envelope. "It's from Sam!" she cried eagerly. "I recognize his handwriting."

"And I've got one from Rob!" said Lisa, crowding in next to Amy and gingerly plucking a white envelope out of her hand. "Thank you, I'll take that!"

Amy was left with two letters. "Sorry there's nothing for you, Shanon," she said. "Both of these are for me."

Shanon sighed. "That's okay. Mars is probably too busy with his pig program."

"Is he still into that?" asked Amy.

Shanon giggled. "I heard from Kate, who heard from Lisa's brother Reggie, that Mars has started a petition at Ardsley to get the pig adopted as the official school mascot."

Lisa howled with laughter. "Oh, my gosh—that would make their football team the Ardsley Piggies!"

"Listen to this!" said Palmer. She stood up and read Sam's letter out loud.

Dear Palmer,

What you did in asking the Alma Student Council to include Brighton High in your play was a really nice thing. Please thank your friend Shanon for what she did, too. I am truly looking forward to meeting you at the shopping mall. After you hear me and the band play, I hope you can stay awhile. My mom says there are a lot of good restaurants in this place! What kind of food do you like? Also, what's your favorite flower? And (besides Sam and The Fantasy) what kind of music do you like best? If you're wondering what I'm planning, it's something special. It's my way of thanking you for trying to get me into the audition. Please write back as soon as you can.

Yours truly,
Sam

"Wow!" said Amy. "Something *special,* huh?"

Palmer batted her big blue eyes. "I'll have to get a new dress!"

"You have tons in your closet," said Shanon.

"Not anymore," said Palmer. "I cut them all up for the quilt!"

"We can discuss your wardrobe later," said Lisa. "First I want to read you Rob's letter."

Dear Lisa,

Thanks for telling me about the auditions for Everypeople. How did the girls' tryouts go? Yesterday we had our

41

auditions over here, and I think I did great! It was a lot more fun than running the 440! When I sang, my voice didn't even crack. I'm keeping my fingers crossed . . . for both of us!

Yours,
Rob

"Wow!" said Amy. "Sounds like he had a good audition."

"I wish Gina would announce the parts," Lisa said nervously. "This suspense is killing me."

"Casting a play is very important," said Shanon. "Gina probably wants to take her time deciding."

"Hey, look at this!" Amy exclaimed as she pulled a square of metallic black cotton out of an envelope. "Evon sent me a piece for the quilt!"

"Wow!" said Shanon. "All the way from Australia!"

"Your friend Evon is so neat," said Lisa, taking the letter from Amy's outstretched hand.

Dear Amy,

When you asked for a piece of cloth from Australia, I thought of the perfect thing. Here is a piece of my first Nick Cave T-shirt. It was getting worn out, and I've got another one! What do you want this for anyway?

How are you and the other Foxes doing? We started a pen pal exchange at our school, and I am currently writing to a boy who lives in England. Too bad he's not closer! Please say hi to Lisa, Palmer, and Shanon. Hope I can come up for another visit to Alma Stephens sometime soon.

Cheerio,
Evon

"Nice letter," said Shanon.

"Nice piece of cloth," said Lisa, putting it down next to the quilt.

"Who's the other letter from, Amy?" Palmer asked.

Amy blushed. "John sent me another poem. It's kind of dedicated to me."

"He dedicated a poem to you!" said Shanon. "Let's hear it!"

Amy cleared her throat and began to read:

> *"A poem for Amy, by John Adams*
> *Every woman*
> *In every way*
> *Teaches man*
> *His place to play*
> *Evermore*
> *Religious*
> *Or*
> *Rude?"*

Lisa laughed. "John Adams is truly obscure! Is that all he wrote?"

"That's all," said Amy. "I guess his *Everypeople* audition didn't go too well. He doesn't even mention it."

Shanon began folding up the Fox quilt. "I wish I had heard from Mars," she said wistfully. "But I'm glad you three got good letters. I think Palmer's is especially exciting."

"Thanks," Palmer said, beaming. "Now all I have to do is get permission to go to Newton."

"You still haven't asked for a pass to the concert?" asked Lisa.

"I was going to do it yesterday," Palmer said, "when I turned in my paper to Miss Grayson. But she was too busy to talk to me. Anyway, she didn't look very cheerful. I thought I'd wait until she was in a better mood."

"Miss Grayson has been looking kind of upset lately," Shanon said. "I guess we all know why."

Lisa shook her head. "Brenda told me she heard that Mr. Griffith was actually applying for jobs in Princeton."

"Princeton!" Shanon moaned. "That's miles from here! No wonder Miss Grayson's unhappy. She probably—"

Shanon broke off at the sound of a quick knock on the door, and Brenda Smith came bounding in. "Somebody just told me that the cast list is up for *Everypeople*!" she cried. "It's on the bulletin board at Booth Hall!"

"Oh, my gosh!" said Lisa. "Who's on the list? Do you know yet?"

"I haven't seen it yet," replied Brenda. "All I know is that Gina Hawkins was on her way to post the announcement five minutes ago."

Amy's heart began to thump. "Let's go," she said.

"I hope you all got parts," Shanon said excitedly.

"Me, too," added Palmer. "I hope that every person who wants to be in *Everypeople* gets in. But now, if you'll excuse me, I'm going to think about what I'm going to wear when I go to see Sam."

Lisa and Amy were already dashing out of the suite, with Brenda close at their heels. They made it over to Booth Hall in record time, but a large crowd had already formed in front of the bulletin board.

"Who's Everyman?" cried Muffin Talbot. The shortest girl in the class, she was jumping up and down trying to see the list.

44

"Some third-form boy I've never heard of," Dolores Countee replied. Lisa stood on tiptoe to peer over the tall redhead's shoulder.

"Excuse me," Amy said, squeezing in. "Can we please see?"

"Oh, my gosh!" screamed Dawn Hubbard. "There's my name!"

"What part did you get?" Muffin asked.

"Home!" said Dawn. "I hope that's one of the characters with a solo!"

Lisa was nervously biting the corner of her bottom lip as she pushed her way to the front. Amy was standing right beside her. There were two cast lists—one for Alma and the other for Ardsley.

"I can't believe it!" Lisa gasped. Rob's name was staring her right in the face. It was on top of the boys' list. "He got the lead!" she cried. "Rob's playing Everyman! I knew it would happen! I knew it!"

"You're not going to believe this either," Amy whispered in a shocked voice. Her eyes were glued to the girls' list. She nudged Lisa. "Look! We—we've both got parts!"

"Yippee!" yelled Lisa, moving over. "That's incredible! Rob and I—"

Her voice broke off sharply when she caught sight of her own name. It was written under the chorus! Her disbelieving eyes flew back to the top of the list. "There must be some mistake!" she gasped.

Amy turned to her, wide-eyed. "I'm in a state of shock, too," she said.

"*You* got it, Amy!" Lisa cried. "*You* got the part of Everywoman! But you weren't even trying out for it!"

Amy smiled sheepishly. "Weird, huh? I guess Gina must

45

have thought I was right for it. Yippee! Isn't this amazing!"

"Yeah," Lisa gulped. "Congratulations." She wanted to be happy for Amy, but it wasn't easy.

"Congratulations, Amy!" Brenda said, coming up behind them. "I got a part, too! I'm playing Soul! It's the part I wanted!"

"It's the part *I* wanted, too," said Amy.

"But you got an even better part," Brenda exclaimed. "You got Everywoman!" Then she turned her blue eyes on Lisa. "Congratulations, Lisa. You're playing Beauty, right?"

Lisa forced a smile.

"You'll probably get a fabulous costume," Brenda said. "With a name like Beauty, they'll have to make you look beautiful."

"Congratulations, everybody!" said Dawn, joining the group. "I'm playing the part of Home. From what I hear, Home is the nicest character in Gina's whole play and instead of singing rock, she sings a folk song."

"Interesting," said Muffin. "I can't wait to read the full script! I'm going to be Accomplishments—whatever that means!"

Lisa felt herself zoning out while the conversation buzzed all around her. Everybody seemed so happy. Even the people who hadn't gotten parts were being good sports about it. But she didn't feel like being a good sport. She was disappointed and even a little embarrassed. She had tried so hard to get the part of Everywoman. She'd even borrowed that Middle Ages costume! And now Amy, who hadn't even *wanted* the part, had gotten it!

"Too bad John didn't make it," Amy said as the crowd began to drift away.

"What?" said Lisa distractedly.

"John didn't get a part," said Amy. "You're lucky Rob did. You'll get to see him all the time at rehearsals."

"I guess," Lisa said, trying to look on the bright side.

Amy touched her arm. "Hey, I'm sorry. I know how much you wanted to be Everywoman."

"Who cares?" bluffed Lisa. "We don't even know what the play is about. We probably never will. It sounds awfully intellectual."

Amy pointed toward the snack bar. "Choc-shot?" she offered. "My treat."

"No thanks," Lisa said, ducking away. "I . . . I've got stuff to do!"

Batting back tears, she dashed out of the building. *At least I got a part!* she thought. *And Rob did, too. Things could always be worse.* But telling herself that didn't make Lisa feel any better. First Shanon had beaten her out for Student Council rep, and now Amy had beaten her out for the part of Everywoman! Worst of all, Amy would be playing opposite Rob! In the play, Everyman and Everywoman were like boyfriend and girlfriend. Now, Rob would be spending all his time pretending to be Amy's boyfriend!

CHAPTER SEVEN

Dear Sam,

    Your letter was so nice. I've been thinking about it a lot. My favorite thing in the world to eat is sweets, so I have to say that my dream meal would consist of all sweet things. I would start with a chocolate sundae and end up with a banana split with pistachio ice cream. Does that sound too gross to you? I hope not. The only other thing I really love is spaghetti. As for my favorite flower, I think white gardenias are perfectly beautiful. We have a lot of them at home in Palm Beach. My mother and I used to wear them in our hair when we went out to dinner together. It was one of the only things we ever totally agreed about. As for your other question, I'm afraid I'm stuck. I have never been much of a music lover. But now that I've heard Sam and The Fantasy, I must say that you are my favorite sound. Sam, this is really nice of you! I've never had anyone plan something this special for me in my life! Write if there's anything else you need to know.

Yours,
Palmer

Dear Palmer,

Thanks for the vital information. There are just a couple more things I need to know. 1. What is your favorite color? 2. What is your favorite constellation of stars? I can't wait until you meet my mom. I told her (joke) that you were my favorite "fantasy." And then I showed her your picture. She said you looked like a nice girl and asked if you were a model. We are having Year Book elections at school this week. The seniors are voting for Best Looking and Most Athletic and things like that. If you went to Brighton, you would be a definite candidate for one of these categories— the first one (no joke!).

Sincerely,
Sam

Dear John,

Have you heard the news? I'm going to be playing the girl lead in Gina Hawkins's new play! This is truly rad since I didn't even think of trying out for it. Gina told me I'll have eight songs to sing! And a lot of them are funny. I'll be singing one to a character named Accomplishments and trying to get her to go to the center of the earth with me.

Accomplishments is going to turn out to be a coward, though.

I saw some of the lyrics for the boys' music, and it's great, too. Rob, who is playing Everyman, gets to sing a really cool song called "Money" to a character named Riches, who drives a sports car. Riches doesn't want to go to the center of the earth either. Nobody does in this play because they think they'll burn up. But actually there's a buried treasure there.

Our first rehearsal is coming up at the end of the week.

Gina's been telling me a lot about the play, but I still haven't seen the script—only some of the song lyrics. Everybody in the cast is beginning to wonder if she's actually written this play. Rumor has it that she's been staying up all night in her room changing it around and around. I definitely would not want to be a playwright! Anyway, it's too bad that you didn't get into this.

Your pen pal,
Amy

P.S. I thought your last poem was truly excellent.

Dear Amy,

   Congratulations. I am not at all surprised that you got the lead. Anybody who's heard you sing knows you have talent. Guess what? I got into the poetry series at Brighton Library. It's turning out to be a much bigger deal than I thought. I get to read six of my poems. The one hitch is that it falls on a reunion weekend, so my dad (who also went to Ardsley) will be coming up. He is not too *thrilled* about my poetry writing. He warned me about wasting my time when I joined the Lit. Mag. He has it figured out that I am going into banking like him. Maybe I will. But I still like writing poetry. I hope he doesn't have a stroke when he hears me at the reading. And I hope you can come to town and be there, too. I definitely want to see you in Everypeople.

Bye for now,
John

Dear Mars,

   Once you said that if I ever had something that was bothering me, I should tell you about it. So I hope you don't

mind if I tell you about something that you may find some-
what boring. It's about two of our teachers. I think you may
have seen them once, when they came to chaperone us at the
dance at Ardsley. Miss Grayson is our French teacher and
lives in our dorm. She is almost like our mother—or actually
our big sister, because she's only in her twenties. Mr. Griffith
is my favorite teacher. He teaches us English. Anyway, they
have been dating. It's probably supposed to be a secret, but
it's one that hasn't been too well kept.

I recently learned that Mr. Griffith is going to be leaving
our school. I don't know why. We are really going to miss
him, but worst of all I think this has upset Miss Grayson a
lot. Yesterday I saw her, and it looked like she'd been crying.
It must be very hard for her. She is a grown-up and supposed
to help us with all our problems, which means she's not
supposed to let anybody know she has any of her own. I feel
it would be poking into her business if we asked her about
this. And I certainly can't talk to Mr. Griffith about his
leaving Alma Stephens—I'm not even supposed to know
about it. So, it seems there's nothing I can do. But I wish
there was. Do you have any ideas?

Sadly,
Shanon

Dear Shanon,
I think you are absolutely right when you say this is none
of your business, but who cares? I can understand your
feeling sorry for your teachers, especially Miss Grayson.
What kind of life will she have teaching the rest of her days
in a girls' school if the guy she's in love with leaves her? It
is heavy. The one thing you could probably do is try to

51

convince Mr. Griffith not to leave Alma Stephens. If he knew how much the students like his teaching, maybe he would stay.

Mars

P.S. Nobody wants a pig as the Ardsley mascot. I am truly disappointed.

Dear Rob,

   I have some disappointing news—if you haven't already heard: I did not get the lead in the play. Amy did! Even so, I am happy that you got the boys' lead. I haven't seen the script yet. Gina has been talking about it to Amy a lot, but since I play such a tiny part, she has not talked to me at all. Anyway, I will do my best to have fun at this. At least I'll be seeing you at rehearsals.

Congratulations,
Lisa

P.S. My character's name is Beauty.

Dear Lisa,

   You're wrong. Your news is not disappointing. I'm just glad you got into the play. I bet your part is a good one, too—Gina made an excellent choice putting you in a part called Beauty. Tell Amy "Way to go, Ho!" She will probably be interesting to work with. She's a neat girl. I like her.

See you soon,
Rob

Dear Mr. Griffith,

   I hope you don't mind my writing to you, but I have heard that you are going to leave Alma Stephens. As you are one of my favorite teachers, I sincerely wish you wouldn't. I was *looking forward to studying with you next year. When I came to Alma, I didn't know how to write a good paragraph. Now I am writing feature articles for* The Ledger! *And all that is thanks to you. I know lots of other students here feel the same way about you. If there is any way you can help it, please don't go.*

Sincerely yours,
Shanon Davis

CHAPTER EIGHT

———◆———

"Shanon, may I have a word with you?"

Shanon glanced uneasily at Mr. Griffith, who was standing next to his desk in the front of the room. English class had just ended, and Lisa, Palmer, and Amy were already at the door.

"We'll meet you behind the gym," called Lisa.

"See you later, then," Shanon said. Avoiding Mr. Griffith's gaze, she fumbled for her books. It had been two days since she'd left the note in his mailbox.

"About the letter you sent me," Mr. Griffith began.

"I know," Shanon blurted out. "It was none of my business."

Mr. Griffith smiled. "You're right. But I still appreciate those nice things you said about me."

Shanon flushed. "You do?"

"What teacher wouldn't?" he replied. "It's great to know that you've actually reached some of your students."

"Oh, you *have*!" Shanon said enthusiastically. "I remember the first class we had with you. You gave us that line from the Robert Frost poem about coming to where two roads meet and not knowing which one to take. We had to write a paragraph on it. It was a hard thing to understand, but you made us jump right in! By the time I finished that paragraph, I had pretty much figured the poem out. By myself! You didn't just come out and explain it to us."

The young English teacher's eyes softened. "Thanks. I'll have to remember to give that assignment to . . . next year's third-form class."

"Does that mean you're not leaving Alma?" Shanon asked hopefully.

Mr. Griffith looked away. "I'm not sure. And I'm really not at liberty to discuss my plans, Shanon. A lot of things are involved."

Shanon looked down at the floor. She wondered what things Mr. Griffith was talking about, but she knew better than to ask.

"I'm not the only one who decides whether I stay or leave," the teacher volunteered lightly. Having cleared his desk, he headed toward the door.

"But all the girls at Alma think you're a great teacher," Shanon said, following behind him.

Mr. Griffith turned and smiled. "That's nice," he said. "That's what I like about teaching—there are big rewards, even if they aren't monetary."

Shanon wanted to ask what Mr. Griffith meant by that remark, but again she decided not to. Maybe his leaving Alma had something to do with his salary.

"How are the costumes going?" Mr. Griffith asked as they walked outside together.

"I'm collecting lots of interesting pieces of material," Shanon told him. "We're sewing them together to make patchwork."

55

"Nice idea," said Mr. Griffith. "I'll look around and see what I have to donate. Maybe some old neckties would be useful."

Shanon's eyes lit up. She'd be glad to have some more fabric for the costumes, but her immediate thought was of the Fox quilt. It would be so great to include something from Mr. Griffith in it. "Thanks," she smiled and said, "that would be wonderful."

"I'll scrounge around in my closet and bring you something tomorrow," Mr. Griffith offered. And turning toward the library, he waved and said, "Now I'm off to do some 'homework' of my own."

Shanon waved back before heading toward the gym. "See you in class tomorrow."

"Righto!" called Mr. Griffith. "And thanks again for your vote of confidence."

Shanon smiled wistfully as she watched him walk away. He was one of the nicest adults she'd ever met. And he'd taught her to love books even more than she already had and to do her favorite thing in the world—to write!

CHAPTER NINE

Lisa's heart began to race as she pushed through the double doors of the theater.

"Isn't this exciting?" said Amy. "Today is the day we're finally going to read Gina's play!"

Lisa scanned the seats for boys, but no Ardies had arrived yet. She could hardly wait to see Rob! Amy went straight up front to talk to Gina, but Lisa slipped into an aisle seat. She wanted to be the first to see Rob when he came in, and she wanted to make sure the two of them sat together.

Reaching up to her long, dark ponytail, Lisa tightened the bright red bow she was wearing. She was also wearing a small white sailor's cap that she'd stenciled herself with blue butterflies. Her short white pants were hand-stenciled as well, and her white T-shirt had the words "I'm cool, how about you?" written on it. Lisa had thought a long time about her outfit. Even if she wasn't the leading lady in the play, she wanted to make sure Rob noticed her. The door in the back swung open and a noisy group of boys spilled into the theater. Lisa's heart jumped as she quickly scanned the group. Rob wasn't there! There was only Bob Brown, the

Ardsley director, and some other boys she'd never seen before.

"We left Williams behind!" Bob Brown announced loudly to Gina as the boys made their way toward the front. "He was in the middle of track practice. The coach promised to get him here."

Lisa couldn't wait for Rob to appear. She closed her eyes and tried to imagine his entrance. He'd be tan, of course, since it was sunny almost every day now, and Rob was a jock who probably spent most of his free afternoons outdoors playing softball or running track. It had been months since she'd last seen him, so his dark curly hair would probably be longer. Maybe he'd even be taller, Lisa thought, turning his image over in her mind. Of course Rob was quite tall already, but boys his age still put on inches in height, just like girls did. Anyway, she told herself, if she knew Rob, he would look super! He'd be wearing a brightly colored polo shirt and a pair of khakis. He'd want to look his best—for *her*! He would walk into the theater and right away he'd see her. He would wave and hurry to the seat she was saving for him. Maybe he would hold her hand, the way he'd done the last time they were together. . . .

Lisa's reverie was shattered by Kate's voice ringing out from the front of the theater. "Come on down, Lisa!" she called. Lisa looked up and saw the stage manager holding a big stack of scripts in her arms. "Get a copy of the play," Kate yelled. "Anybody else who doesn't have one, line up, also."

Lisa left her seat reluctantly. Since she hadn't gotten a big role, her enthusiasm for Gina's play had diminished greatly. Now all she really hoped to get out of it was a chance to see Rob at rehearsals. Kate was just giving her one of the fat, blue-covered scripts when the doors in the back opened again. Out of the corner of her eye, Lisa saw a boy come dashing in and almost trip over his own feet.

"Oops!" he said loudly. "Just thought I'd drop in. See you next fall!"

The Ardsley boys began to laugh good-naturedly. Lisa did a double take and looked at the boy again. It was Rob—and she hadn't even recognized him! His long dark curls had been cut off in a flat top!

"Uh, excuse the outfit," he muttered, glancing down at his beat-up old running clothes. "I came straight from track practice. I didn't want to miss anything."

"You look great, Rob!" Gina called out cheerfully. "Come on in!"

"Hey, man!" Amy called cheerfully. She was still standing onstage next to Gina. "Or should I say *Every*man?"

The Ardsley crew started laughing again, and some of the girls begin to titter.

"Way to go, Everyman!" Bob Brown said.

Looking embarrassed but pleased, Rob made a beeline for the stage. He passed Lisa by without a glance. She started to say something but then stopped herself. If he wasn't even going to bother looking for her, she certainly wasn't going to throw herself at *him*. Besides, she wasn't sure she liked his flat top anyway. Tucking the script under her arm, she began making her way toward the back of the theater again. Suddenly she felt a tap on her shoulder.

Lisa turned around impatiently—and her heart skipped a beat.

"Hey," Rob said, flashing a happy grin. Lisa had always really liked the way he smiled.

"Uh, hi," she said, trying to sound cool.

59

"I didn't recognize you in that sailor outfit," Rob teased, his dark blue eyes twinkling. "Going on a cruise?"

Lisa flushed. "What happened to your hair?" she said bluntly.

Now it was Rob's turn to look embarrassed. "It's the latest. Don't you like it?"

"Everybody down front!" Kate called impatiently before Lisa could think of a reply. Rob took Lisa's hand for a moment and pulled her down the aisle.

"Let's sit here," Lisa said, pointing to two seats.

"That's no good," Kate butted in. "Rob has to sit next to Amy, and you're supposed to sit with the chorus."

Lisa rolled her eyes. It was bad enough she wouldn't be playing opposite Rob, now she wasn't even going to be allowed to sit next to him!

Gina stood up in front of the group and clapped for attention. "If everyone has a script, let's get started!" she said. "Nobody's seen the whole script before, and I've never heard it. So we're all in this together. Bob Brown will be playing some of the musical numbers on the piano, and we'll have guitar accompaniment for the others."

Brenda Smith's hand shot up. "How many rehearsals are we going to have?"

"Lots," Gina said. "And that goes for the boys, too."

"What do you mean?" Lisa asked. "Won't we all be rehearsing together?"

Gina threw up her arms helplessly. "Sometimes yes," she said. "And sometimes no. The schedules were just too complicated to coordinate more than four joint rehearsals," she explained. "So the boys will have to rehearse a lot at Ardsley with Bob, while the girls will be working here with me."

"Isn't that going to be a problem?" said Amy.

"Not for the chorus members," Gina replied. "Most of the girls' scenes take place among themselves and with Everywoman. The same goes for the boys' scenes. They're mainly just written for boy characters—and with Everyman, of course."

"What is this, separation of the sexes?" a tall, skinny Ardie quipped. "I thought this play was co-ed!" Everyone started to giggle.

"Calm down," said Gina. "There are a few boy-girl scenes among the chorus members. And there are lots of them between the two leads, which means that Rob and Amy will have to have a bunch of extra rehearsals together."

Some hoots came from the Ardsley section. "Way to go, Williams! Private rehearsals!"

Lisa felt her face getting hot. "Could we get on with the reading?" she asked.

"Sure thing," Gina replied seriously. "Turn to Act One, Scene One, everybody. . . ."

The first part of the play seemed endless to Lisa. She only had three lines. Of course she would also be singing with the girls' chorus, but nobody knew the music yet. Amy and Rob—along with Brenda who was playing Soul, the narrator—were in just about every scene. Lisa skimmed ahead in the script while the other actors were reading. The play actually seemed pretty clever. As far as she could make out, Everyman and Everywoman had to go on separate trips to the center of the earth, where Soul had said they'd find treasure. They could each take three companions. Everyman took Riches, Good Times, and Courage. Everywoman chose Accomplishments, Pride, and Heart. Lisa kept skimming the script to find out where her part came in again. She sighed and closed it over her thumb. As far as she could tell, Beauty was hardly in the whole play.

"Okay, everybody. That's the end of the first half!" Gina finally announced. "Take ten!"

"Ten-minute break!" Kate cried.

The cast got up to stretch, and several of them began to wander outdoors. Keeping her eyes on Rob, Lisa stayed in her seat.

"There you are," he said, tapping her sailor hat.

"You read your part well," Lisa said. "I sort of lost track of what happened in the middle, but you were great in the beginning."

"You were, too," Rob said.

"How can you say that?" Lisa scoffed. "I only had three lines."

"You'll be onstage a lot of the time, though," Rob reminded her. "You'll have a lot of silent acting."

Lisa tossed her head. "You're just trying to make me feel better."

"Since when is that a crime?" Rob asked, kneeling down next to her and squeezing her hand.

With a happy smile, Lisa squeezed back. But then Rob abruptly pulled his hand away as Amy came over, her dark eyes flashing with excitement. "Isn't this awesome?" she said. "I think this play could go on Broadway!"

Lisa chuckled. "Broadway? Let's not get carried away."

"I wouldn't put it down," Rob said, standing up next to Amy. "It's pretty amazing for somebody our age to write a two-act musical."

"I wasn't putting it down," Lisa protested. She glanced at Rob and Amy. How could they understand? There was no way she could be as enthusiastic as they were when she had such a small part. She was barely even *in* the play.

Lisa was about to try explaining that when Rob suddenly turned away and faced Amy. "John said to say hi." he told her.

"Say hi to him back," Amy replied with a happy grin.

Rob grinned, too, as Amy rattled on. "Isn't it fantastic that John got into the poetry reading?"

"He deserves it," Rob said. "And he wants you to come to the reading."

Lisa's heart sank. She and Rob only had ten minutes together, and he was spending it all with Amy!

"Everybody in the theater!" Kate announced. "We're going to read the second act now!"

Lisa groaned as Rob disappeared with Amy. Then she scooted over so that Muffin and Dawn could take their seats with the chorus.

"Where's Beauty in this play?" Lisa hissed to Dawn.

"She has a fantastic monologue at the end," Dawn whispered back. "I looked at the script outside. It's a good part—really!"

Lisa perked up. Maybe everything would be okay after all. But as the second act progressed, most of the action seemed to take place between Rob and another boy called Courage. Then Amy had some scenes with a character named Heart. Heart and Courage were the only two friends who did not desert them in their journey to the center of the earth. Suddenly the word *Beauty* loomed in front of Lisa's eyes. Here it was—finally—her big scene with Everyman! Having come to the center of the earth, Everyman had found his treasure!

Lisa read the scene with Rob, her voice filled with emotion. "*I* am the treasure!" she cried. "*I* am Beauty! It is I whom you seek! Take me with you!"

Lisa's heart soared as she read her lines. It was like a dream come true—she and Rob on stage together!

But the dream was over far too soon. The play kept going, with no more big moments for Beauty. Lisa's thoughts began to drift again, as Amy read scene after scene with other members of the chorus. Lisa yawned dispiritedly. Suddenly, a wave of tittering swept through the theater. Lisa looked over at Dawn's script.

"What's so funny?" she whispered. "What page are we on?"

"Seventy-three," Dawn said softly.

Lisa quickly flipped through her script. There, on the bottom of page 73, in big bold letters were the stage directions: THEY KISS.

"Who kisses?" Lisa blurted out.

"Rob and Amy," Brenda squealed.

Rob blushed and turned to Gina. "Are you sure about this?"

"What's the matter, Williams," yelled a skinny Ardie, "don't you believe in kissing girls?"

Rob turned redder. "Not in public."

"But in private it's okay, huh?" Brenda teased.

Everyone but Lisa started to laugh. Even Amy, though she looked embarrassed, seemed to be enjoying the joke.

"The kiss is only a symbolic one," Gina broke in matter-of-factly. "Everyman and Everywoman have a lot to be happy about at this point! Besides, they haven't seen each other in a long time. This is something they've been looking forward to."

"Right!" one of the girls giggled. "After a hard day's work looking for treasure, there's nothing like a nice kiss!"

Everyone started laughing again, and even Gina began to look flustered. "Listen, everyone," she called out above the noise. "It's okay to poke fun. I don't mind it, especially at the first rehearsal. I didn't say this play was perfect. But I wrote it the best way I knew how. So from now on, I hope you can trust me, and we can all work hard on it together."

The cast quieted down.

"Sorry. I didn't mean to rib you," the outspoken Ardie apologized.

"I think the kiss is a nice touch," Amy said kindly.

Gina smiled. "Thanks, you guys. And thanks for a good reading. Let's keep going. We're almost at the end. And then Bob will play the finale for you. It's a real heavy number, and I think you're going to like it."

Everyone buckled down to the script again—everyone, that is, but Lisa. Any concentration she'd had was totally shot. She couldn't believe the way this play was turning out! It was one thing for Amy to be Rob's leading lady, but now he was actually going to *kiss* her! *Rob's never even kissed me!* Lisa thought miserably. She forced her gaze down onto the script, but she couldn't read a word. Her eyes were too filled with tears.

CHAPTER TEN

"I think I know what Mr. Griffith was talking about," Kate said soberly when Shanon recounted her after-class conversation with the English teacher. The two girls were in *The Ledger* office, busy getting out the latest issue of the newspaper.

"What?" Shanon asked eagerly.

"Every three years the faculty comes up for review," Kate explained. "Maybe this is Mr. Griffith's year."

"What does that mean?" said Shanon.

"It means that if Miss Pryn and the rest of the administration aren't satisfied with his teaching, they may not ask him to come back next year."

"That's horrible!" Shanon said. "How could they do that? What does Miss Pryn know about Mr. Griffith's teaching anyway?"

Kate shrugged. "I've never seen her visit a single class since I've been at Alma. Maybe the head of the English department . . ."

But Shanon wasn't listening. She was already trying to figure out a way to help. "When do we have to get this copy to the printer?" she broke in.

"It's late already," Kate replied mournfully. "We'd better finish up here or Dolores will be on our case."

Shanon rolled her eyes. Dolores Countee was the editor-in-chief of *The Ledger*. But her main role, it sometimes seemed to Shanon, was telling everyone else what to do. As far as Shanon could tell, it was Kate, as Dolores's assistant, who did most of the real work.

"Where *is* Dolores?" asked Shanon.

Kate looked up from a stack of photographs. "She was supposed to meet with Miss Pryn this morning. She's the student rep to the administration, remember? She was planning to ask Miss Pryn about the possibility of having more four-o'clocks."

"That's just what we need in this school—more tea times in the library," Shanon burst out. "Why can't Dolores talk to Miss Pryn about *real* issues?"

"Like Mr. Griffith?" Kate asked.

"Yes," Shanon said, edging over toward the computer. She looked from the keyboard to Kate and back again, then took a deep breath and said, "Is there any way we can squeeze in another article? What have we got in the 'Leave It to Wanda' column?"

"A bit about Class Day," Kate replied. "I wrote it. And if I say so myself, it's pretty funny."

"Ummm," said Shanon, "Class Day isn't till next month. Would you mind if I put something else in the column?"

Kate gave her a knowing look. "About Mr. Griffith?"

Shanon nodded. "We can't just let the best teacher in school get fired. We have to do something about it!"

"It would be one way of showing Miss Pryn how popular Mr. Griffith is," Kate agreed. "But Dolores isn't here to approve the switch."

"Precisely," said Shanon. "Dolores *isn't* here. That puts you in charge. *You're* the assistant editor!"

Kate adjusted her glasses. "That's right! I'm the *assistant* editor. And you know how Dolores likes to have the final okay on everything in *The Ledger.*"

"But this is for Mr. Griffith," Shanon pleaded. "So what if Dolores hasn't seen the column. What can she do to us anyway? If she gets mad, you can blame it on me."

Kate was already shaking her head *no,* but she took one look at Shanon's hopeful face and changed her mind. "Okay," she said decisively. "Start writing!"

Before Kate could change her mind again, Shanon sat down at the computer and got to work. The words seemed to flow across the screen. She'd never written so fast or so well in her life.

Leave It to Wanda

Wanda can't be too funny this week—there's something serious she needs to discuss. Like how come her favorite English teacher is being taken away from her. Sure, the administration is the one who hires and fires around here. But does the administration ever sit in the classrooms? The answer is no. So how can the administration say if a teacher is a good or bad one.

Not naming any names, but this particular teacher is the best that Wanda's ever had. Instead of giving loads of homework and boring assignments, he makes each class a learning experience. Like the time he asked somebody in class to lie down on the floor and pretend to be the dead body of Julius Caesar. Or the time he had everyone act out their book reports instead of reading them.

After the class when she had to pretend to be Julius Caesar's dead body while everyone else was standing around her and reading scenes from the Shakespearean play of the same name, Wanda really knew what the playwright was talking about. And the day everybody acted out their book reports, Wanda couldn't wait to leave class and get to the library so she could check out the books her classmates had read. These two classes could have been boring, but instead they are events that Wanda will never forget.

So before the administration starts giving faculty members a bad review because of their teaching, maybe it should speak to the students. They are the only ones who really know what goes on in the classroom. In closing, Wanda has just one thing to say: If you let this teacher go, the administration should go back to school itself and learn what a good education is all about!

"Miss Grayson?" Palmer walked hesitantly into the office of the French department, where Maggie Grayson was hurriedly gathering up some papers at a desk.

"Hi, Palmer," she said. "What can I do for you?"

Palmer put on her best smile. "Can I talk with you for a minute?"

"Sorry," Miss Grayson said. "It's after office hours, and I'm on my way to an appointment. Can't it wait until later?"

"I'll make it quick," Palmer promised. "I was just wondering if you'd marked my French paper yet."

Smiling, Miss Grayson produced a paper with a big A-minus on it. "It was excellent," she said. "You've made great progress."

Palmer beamed proudly. "Thanks. I was hoping you'd say that. So I hope you won't mind giving me an off-campus pass."

Miss Grayson looked puzzled. "What does my giving you a pass have to do with your homework?"

Palmer blushed. "I just thought if you saw I was making such a good effort you might allow me, uh, a privilege."

The teacher gave her a questioning look. "Okay, Palmer," she said. "Out with it. . . ."

Palmer bit her lip. She knew she was asking for a big favor. But she was sure Miss Grayson would say yes once she realized how important it was.

"I have this friend," Palmer began. "He's a musician, and he's going to be in a concert. His mother will be driving him and his band there. Anyway, may I go?"

Miss Grayson shrugged. "I don't see why not. You have one more town pass coming, don't you?"

"I do have a pass coming," Palmer hedged, "but this concert isn't actually in town. It's in a shopping mall. As I said, the boy's mother will be driving us there."

"What shopping mall?" Miss Grayson asked.

"In Newton." Palmer swallowed hard, waiting for her teacher's response.

Miss Grayson looked puzzled. "You don't mean Newton, Massachusetts?"

Palmer nodded. "It's not that far away, really."

"But it's out of state," Miss Grayson said. "I can't give you permission to go out of state."

"Yes, you can," pleaded Palmer. "Dolores went to a

70

fraternity dance in New Jersey just a few weeks ago!"

"But Dolores is an upperclassman," Miss Grayson reminded her gently. "I'm afraid third formers are not allowed out of state."

Palmer began to breathe hard. "I never heard of that rule before."

"I'm sorry," Miss Grayson repeated, "but it's always been on the books."

"But this is going to be something really special," cried Palmer. "It's something I *can't* miss! You *have* to let me go!"

"I can understand how disappointed you are," Miss Grayson said sympathetically, "but it's out of the question."

"I already told him I'd be there," Palmer exclaimed.

Miss Grayson shook her head sadly. "You shouldn't have done that. Not until you'd gotten permission."

Palmer glared at Miss Grayson. "I should have known!" she said angrily.

"Known what?" Miss Grayson asked.

Tears of anger welled up in Palmer's eyes. "I should have known that no matter how good my French paper was, you wouldn't let me go! And just because this boy doesn't go to Ardsley!"

Miss Grayson sighed. "That has nothing to do with it. I don't even know who your friend is."

"His name is Sam O'Leary," Palmer said shrilly, "and everyone here is against him and me. First Miss Pryn said he couldn't be in the play, and now this! I thought you were different, but you're just like her! I wish I'd never come to Alma Stephens!"

Leaving the French teacher speechless, Palmer fled from the office, ran across the quad, and threw herself under a tree. The tears she'd been holding back spilled down her cheeks.

Now what have I done? she thought miserably. Not only was she going to miss her "dream date" with Sam, but Miss Grayson would probably never forgive her for what she'd said.

While Palmer was outside sobbing, Amy was in the suite, happily sewing a piece on the Fox quilt. As she stitched, she sang one of her songs from the play:

> *"Everyman, Everychild, Everywoman walk a mile*
> *speak ever so softly*
> *We're the ones who pay the rent*
> *It's our home, though heaven sent*
> *We get what we're after. . . .*
> *So leave the waves crystalline pure*
> *Let the mystery remain*
> *Don't rename what can endure*
> *Everybody—"*

Amy broke off at the sound of the suite door slamming behind Palmer. "What's wrong with you?" she asked.

"I had a fight with Miss Grayson," Palmer moaned.

"What?" Amy cried, putting down the quilt.

"It's a long story," Palmer said, curling up on the loveseat. "But the punch line is that I can't go to meet Sam."

"Rats," said Amy. "That's too bad."

"It's worse than bad," Palmer sniffed. "When Miss Grayson told me I couldn't go, I lost my temper. Now I'll probably never get to go anywhere—unless they kick me out of school altogether!"

Amy sat down beside her. "I'm sure it's not that serious. Maybe you could explain—"

72

"Not now," Palmer sighed. "Now I just need a nice long nap. Pass me the quilt?"

"You can't sleep with it," Amy said. "It's not finished yet."

"When *is* it going to be finished?" Palmer grumbled. "It's big enough for two twin beds already. Anyway, who's going to get it when it is finished? We can't *all* sleep under it."

"I don't know," Amy replied. "Maybe we'll have to draw straws. Maybe—"

Once again Amy was interrupted by the sound of a slamming door. This time it was Shanon who stalked into the room. "I did something that's going to get me into a lot of trouble," she said defiantly, "but I don't care."

"You did?" Palmer said, sitting up. "Me, too. What did you do?"

Shanon waved a piece of computer printout paper under her suitemate's nose. "It's a 'Leave It to Wanda' column," she explained. "There's a message to the administration in it. I told them they shouldn't fire Mr. Griffith!"

"Good for you!" exclaimed Amy.

Shanon suddenly looked a little frightened. "Do you think I'll get in trouble for it?" she asked nervously. "It's very critical of Miss Pryn."

"So what!" Amy declared. "There is freedom of the press in this country, you know—even at Alma!"

"Hi, everybody," Lisa said, strolling into the suite with a handful of letters. "Mail for you, Amy," she announced.

"Thanks," Amy said, grabbing an envelope. "It's from John."

Lisa's eyes narrowed. "Lucky you. Rob hasn't written a line since the rehearsal."

73

Shanon glanced up at her. "You sound like you're in a bad mood," she said.

"I am," Lisa replied, kicking off her shoes.

"That makes three of us," Palmer announced.

Amy sighed. "No, make that four," she said, still holding John's letter. "What a bummer!"

"What's wrong?" Lisa asked curiously.

"Yes, tell us," said Shanon.

"See for yourself," Amy offered, handing Shanon the letter.

Dear Amy,

Enclosed is a flyer for my poetry reading. I am getting totally psyched for this. I heard from Rob that you are making an excellent Everywoman. Anyway, I hope you can make it to the reading. You'll be able to meet my dad at the same time because he'll be there, too.

Yours truly,
John

Amy passed around the flyer.

"Why is this a bummer?" Shanon asked. "I think it's excellent that John's going to be in a poetry reading—and that he wants to introduce you to his father."

"Yes, it *is* excellent," said Amy. "Too bad I won't be able to go."

"How come?" asked Palmer. "Don't tell me Miss Grayson won't give you a pass either."

"That's not it," said Amy. "Look at the date! John's poetry reading is the very same day as the play!"

"What a shame," said Shanon.

"Of all the rotten luck!" Amy moaned. "I would give anything to be able to hear John read his poetry."

"Then go!" Palmer said. "All you have to do is drop out of the play."

Amy's mouth fell open. "How could I do that? Gina's depending on me, and so is the rest of the cast. They could never get anybody else to do the part."

"Why not?" Lisa piped up. "I could do it."

Amy's face darkened. "Thanks for the offer. But this play is important to me. I love acting in it."

"So I've noticed," Lisa said snidely.

"What's that supposed to mean?" Amy demanded.

"It means . . ." Lisa sputtered, "that I think you 'love' some of the parts of this play an awful lot. Maybe too much for everybody's good."

Amy threw up her arms. "Will someone tell me what she's talking about. Of course I love the part. It's a challenge."

"And . . . and it's also opposite Rob!" Lisa accused her.

Amy shrugged. "So what?"

"So, I don't see why you have to kiss him in the play," Lisa blurted out. "I think it's really mean."

"*I* didn't write the script," Amy countered. "Anyway, I haven't kissed him yet. That's not going to happen until the last rehearsal. That's the only time Gina said we'll be rehearsing that."

"And then you'll be doing it again at the performance," Lisa reminded her. "And Rob is *my* friend! It isn't fair!"

"The kiss is just symbolic," Amy pleaded. "I have nothing to do with it. Rob probably doesn't even like the idea."

"He'd better not!" Lisa exclaimed, on the verge of tears now. "I think it's terrible!"

Amy grabbed her guitar. "I'm sorry you're so upset about it," she said. "But it's not my fault. Anyway, what happens in *Everypeople* isn't real life—it's only a play."

"Amy's right, Lisa," Shanon said gently. "You should try not to let it bother you."

"Well, it does bother me!" Lisa said hotly.

"The kiss isn't significant," Amy insisted. "It doesn't mean a thing!"

"When somebody kisses my pen pal when I haven't even kissed him myself yet, it certainly *is* significant!" Lisa disagreed.

"This is a stupid argument," said Amy. "I'm getting out of here. It's bad enough I have to miss my pen pal's reading, without one of my best friends acting like she can't trust me."

"Trust has nothing to do with it," said Lisa.

"It has everything to do with it," said Amy, marching toward the door. "I'll see you later. I've got songs to practice."

Shanon and Palmer raised their eyebrows as Amy stormed out of the suite. Lisa scrunched up on the loveseat and flung a cushion onto the floor.

There was a moment of silence, and then Palmer said, "Wow! Amy looked mad."

"The kiss really isn't her fault, Lisa," Shanon said hesitantly.

"I should have known you two wouldn't understand either," Lisa snapped. Then she got up from the loveseat and marched into her bedroom.

"Everyone's going crazy around here," Shanon moaned, nervously folding the quilt.

"I know what you mean," Palmer said sadly. "Once we

were all so happy. Now I'll never know what the special surprise was that Sam was planning, Amy can't go to John's poetry reading, and Lisa's mad at everybody." She strolled over to the window and sighed. "It must be something in the stars!"

CHAPTER ELEVEN

———◆———

Dear Sam,

This is a heartbreaking letter. I have to tell you that I can't make it to the concert. Not only that, I have to confess I hadn't even asked for permission when I accepted your invitation in the first place. I'm terribly sorry. This is just another example of how much they are against public school boys at Alma. I have a plan to write an anonymous letter to "Leave It to Wanda," the student column in our newspaper. Shanon wrote one, and because of it, I think that our favorite teacher, Mr. Griffith (who was getting fired), may not be fired after all. Sorry again about breaking our date. I can't say when the next opportunity will come. But if you're still interested, my favorite colors are blue and yellow, and the Big Dipper is my favorite constellation.

Fondly,
Palmer

Dear Palmer,

It is definitely a drag that we can't meet at the concert. But to tell the truth, my mom wasn't surprised that your school

won't let you go to Newton with us. She thought it was kind
of far away without asking your parents. Don't worry. The
day will come for sure when we can get together and I can
wow you with my special surprise. Last night I checked out
the Big Dipper. It's beautiful, just like you.

Sam O'Leary

Dear Mars,

Things are really weird here in our suite. There's a lot of
tension between Amy and Lisa, but please don't tell Rob
because it's all because of him. I never thought Lisa would
be the kind of girl to get jealous, but she is. I used to think
of her as the happiest and most secure person I know,
someone to look up to. But lately I've been changing my
mind. I'd like to help her, but I don't know how. In fact, I
don't seem to be doing anything all that well, lately. I hate
to say this, but I'm afraid I've bitten off more than I can
chew by volunteering to do the costumes for Everypeople.
The patchwork costumes that Gina designed are really
elaborate. I don't know how I'll ever get them done before
the play opens, even though I have a lot of other girls helping
me.

I hope you can check out Everypeople. It's really interesting. And in spite of Lisa and Amy being mad at each
other, they are both doing a very good job. I took your
advice and tried to show Mr. Griffith how much we like him
at Alma. I even wrote a column for our school paper saying
what a good teacher he is. But speaking of writing, I'd better
stop now and start studying for Friday's biology test.

Yours truly,
Shanon

Dear Shanon,

It sounds like you've got a lot on your brain these days. Maybe you should drop one of the things you're doing. Or ask Gina to make the Everypeople costumes less complicated. And how come they have to be made out of patched together material? Who are you, anyway?—that girl in Rumpelstiltskin who had to make her own thread? Wish I could be there to help you. It's too bad the Foxes aren't getting along these days. You four are the coolest girls at Alma.

Yours,
Mars

Dear John,

I'm very sorry, but I will not be able to come to your poetry reading. It falls on the same afternoon as Everypeople. Is there any other way I can hear what you are doing? Maybe you could send me a tape or I could come to a rehearsal? I really feel bad about this, but I'm enjoying my part in the play and don't want to give it up. I hope you understand.

Sincerely,
Amy

Dear Amy,

Of course I understand why you can't make the reading. I feel bad that I won't be able to see you in the play either. There's going to be a run-through of the poetry reading at the library the day before it takes place. Maybe you could get a pass and come. My dad won't be there, but that's probably just as well. I might be kind of nervous when he's around since he doesn't approve of my writing poetry.

Your pen pal,
John

Dear Rob,
   I have something to ask you—

Dear Rob,
   This may sound dumb, but—

Dear Rob,
   What do you think about kissing Amy in the—

Dear Rob,
   How are you? I am fine. Can't wait until I see you at the next rehearsal. What are your opinions of Everypeople? Your honest opinions?

Yours truly,
Lisa

Dear Lisa,
   I think Everypeople is a cool play. I am amazed at your suitemate Amy and what a good actress and singer she is. See you soon. I can't write any more because I have a Latin test tomorrow.

Best wishes,
Rob

CHAPTER TWELVE

Leave It to Wanda

What's in a preppie? Wanda would like to know because the boy she is currently trying to date is *not* one. He lives in Brighton, and everybody calls him a townie because he goes to the public high school. But does everyone know that Brighton High has one of the best science departments in the state and that a large percentage of their class gets into the best colleges? So, maybe hanging around a townie might be a good idea in some cases. That's what Wanda thinks. Last month Wanda wanted her boyfriend to try out for a play here at Alma, but he was turned down flat. This month Wanda wanted to go on a date with her friend, but she wasn't allowed to. Why not. . . ? Because they weren't going to some dance at Ardsley Academy together, that's why not! It was to someplace more ordinary, like a shopping mall. Every nice boy in the world does not go to

Ardsley Academy. It's time the administration found that out and changed its snobbish policy!

"Did Palmer write this by herself?" Amy asked incredulously.

"Well, I helped her some," Shanon admitted, looking up from Dawn Hubbard's sewing machine. "Why is the needle always coming out of this?" she grumbled, turning her attention back to the borrowed machine.

"Maybe you should go over to the Home Ec department and use one of theirs," Amy suggested.

"How can I with all this stuff?" wailed Shanon, waving at the messy room in frustration. The sitting-room floor was almost completely covered by costumes and bits and pieces of multicolored material. "Where's Kate?" she cried. "She promised to help me."

Amy looked around at the mess. "I can help out some— but only for about an hour."

"Thanks," said Shanon helplessly. "I'll try to fix the sewing machine. You lay out some more material and start cutting it from that pattern."

Just then Palmer burst into the room and dropped her cardigan and book bag on the floor. "You won't *believe* what I just saw!" she shrieked.

"Will you please calm down?" Shanon mumbled. "I can't think straight. And get your stuff off my stuff."

"What's wrong with her?" Palmer asked nonchalantly.

"Shanon's trying to fix the sewing machine," Amy started to explain. "She—"

But Palmer had already run over to the window and was looking out. "They're still there!" she cried. "Come see!"

Amy crossed over, and Shanon reluctantly followed.

"It's Miss Grayson and Mr. Griffith," said Amy. "They look really happy."

"Maybe they're dating again," Shanon said hopefully.

"Darn it," Palmer muttered. "You can't see her hand."

Shanon gave her a puzzled look. "Miss Grayson's hand? What about it?"

"Let's go outside," Palmer said mischievously. "That way you can see for yourself."

Amy giggled. "We're going to go down and stare at Miss Grayson's hand?"

"Come on!" said Palmer. "They're walking away. Let's follow them!"

"But the costumes . . ." groaned Shanon.

"You need a break," Amy said, catching her roommate's excitement. "Let's go see what Palmer's so excited about. We can head off toward the snack bar, and if we happen to pass Maggie and Dan in some romantic spot along the way—" Amy broke off, giggling.

"Then we'll just take a look at Miss Grayson's finger," Shanon finished for her.

The three girls shot out of the suite and down the stairs of the dormitory. As they dashed through the front door, they bumped smack into Lisa.

"Where are you going?" she asked, peering at them over an armful of books.

"To see Miss Grayson and Mr. Griffith," Amy said awkwardly. The two girls avoided each other's eyes.

"Miss Grayson's got something on her finger," Shanon added in an excited voice. "Follow us!"

Lisa dumped her books on the front stoop and took off after her suitemates. "What do you mean she has something on her finger?" she asked, getting caught up in

Shanon's excitement. "Is she wearing false nails?"

"Do you think we'd be so excited about that?" Palmer demanded, taking the lead. "Come on—before we lose them!"

As the four girls sped across the quad, they spied Miss Grayson and Mr. Griffith under a tree just outside Booth Hall.

They ducked under another tree at a safe distance.

"What do we do now?" Shanon whispered.

Lisa and Amy burst into giggles. Palmer's daffy adventure was making them forget they were mad at each other, at least for the moment.

"We'll just walk over, say hi, and look at her finger," Palmer replied.

"Why?" Lisa insisted.

"If you must know," Palmer said, unable to keep her secret any longer, "I went down to Miss Grayson's apartment a little while ago and—"

"How come?" Shanon interrupted.

Palmer blushed. "I had something to say to her, but I couldn't talk because Mr. Griffith was there!"

Lisa gasped. "Mr. Griffith was in her *apartment*? What was he doing there?"

"Having tea, I guess," Palmer said with a shrug. "I saw the cups."

"It looks as if they're having a pretty intense conversation right now," Amy said, keeping an eye on the teachers.

Shanon sighed. "Maggie and Dan make such a cute couple!"

"Let's go say hello to them," Palmer prodded. "I want you to see for yourself what—"

"Uh-oh," said Lisa, "they've seen us."

Still under the tree, Miss Grayson and Mr. Griffith were looking right at the four girls.

"They're coming this way," Amy said uncomfortably.

"Gee," Shanon gulped, "I hope they didn't notice us following them."

"Oh, I'm sure they didn't," Palmer said weakly. "And even if they did, at least you'll get to see—"

"Are you ladies tailing us?" Mr. Griffith said, turning his deep green eyes on the group. While the girls had been discussing the situation, the two teachers had walked right up to them.

Shanon blushed. "Well . . . we. . . ."

"Not exactly," hedged Palmer.

Lisa nudged Amy, her big brown eyes practically bugging out. On Miss Grayson's left ring finger was a beautiful pear-shaped diamond!

"I . . . excuse me," Lisa muttered. "Your ring. . . . I was just—"

"You four are very quick to catch on to things," Miss Grayson broke in with a laugh while Mr. Griffith smiled broadly.

"Does this mean . . . you're engaged?" Shanon asked shyly.

The two teachers beamed at each other.

"That's exactly what it means," Miss Grayson said. "And you're four of the first to hear the news."

"Yippee!" cried Lisa. "Fantastic!"

"Congratulations," said Amy.

"When are you going to get married?" Shanon ventured.

"Hold on, girls," Mr. Griffith said with a laugh. "We scarcely know that ourselves."

Palmer shook the French teacher's hand. "I think it's great news."

Miss Grayson's eyes twinkled. "Thanks. I'm glad you're so happy for us. But I got a feeling you weren't so happy a while ago when you knocked on my door. Was there something you wanted to talk about?"

"It was kind of private," said Palmer.

"Want to tell me now?" Miss Grayson asked, pulling Palmer aside.

Palmer took a breath. "Actually, I wanted to say I was sorry for being so rude to you. I know it isn't really your fault that I can't go to the concert with Sam O'Leary. I figured out that it must be the administration's policy."

"It *is* the policy of the administration to make sure our girls are safe and nearby the school," said Miss Grayson. "Next time, perhaps Sam will ask you to some event right in town, and you can see him then."

"Really?" Palmer said, brightening. "You mean I could go out with him even though he's a townie?"

Miss Grayson looked puzzled. "Of course. That wasn't the reason I didn't give you the pass. You're free to invite your friend to the next Alma event, too, as long as you merit the privilege."

"Invite Sam here?" said Palmer. "What a good idea! There's something coming up really soon I could invite him to—the *Everypeople* play!"

Miss Grayson smiled and nodded. "Sounds like a good idea to me." Then her smile widened as Mr. Griffith joined them.

"We'd better get over to Miss Pryn's, Maggie," he said. "You know how she hates being kept waiting."

"Wow," Lisa murmured. "We have to make sure not to keep *you* waiting when we come to English class, and *you* have to make sure you don't mess up with *Miss Pryn*!"

Mr. Griffith smiled again. "Miss Pryn is a wonderful woman. She sets a fine example for all of us."

"I don't think she's so wonderful," Shanon piped up. "Not if she's going to fire you."

Mr. Griffith and Miss Grayson exchanged glances.

"I read last week's 'Leave It to Wanda' column," Mr. Griffith said. "The one about the faculty member who's supposedly being fired."

Shanon blushed.

"I have a pretty good idea who wrote it," Mr. Griffith continued.

"Okay," Shanon confessed, "it was me. I just hope Miss Pryn read it, too."

Mr. Griffith put a hand on her shoulder. "I was touched by the column, Shanon. Just as I was touched by your letter. I'm glad you value my teaching so highly. But you've got it all wrong. Miss Pryn isn't trying to fire me."

Shanon blanked. "She's not?"

"Then why are you leaving?" Lisa piped up.

"That's right," said Amy. "How come you're looking for another job?"

"Because I think it may be time for me to move on," Mr. Griffith explained gently. "In any case, if I do leave, it won't be because I'm being booted out. And it certainly won't be because I don't feel appreciated here." He put his arm around Miss Grayson's shoulder, and the two teachers turned away.

"Wow," sighed Lisa. "What a great couple."

"Yes, they are," Shanon said softly. "When I grow up, I want to be just like them."

"Me, too," Amy agreed. "But now—let's eat."

There was still time before Amy and Lisa's rehearsal for the four friends to visit the snack bar. They ordered their usual fare—choc-shots—except for Shanon, who took a vanilla shake.

"I can't afford to eat any more chocolate," she sighed, with an envious glance at Lisa's drink. "The way my face has been breaking out lately, I've got to stick with vanilla."

"Here's to Maggie and Dan," Amy said, raising her glass.

Palmer giggled. "I'll drink to that! And to Miss Grayson's suggestion that I invite Sam to the play!"

"Great idea," Lisa said agreeably. "Then all of our pen pals will be around on the same night."

"Not John," Amy corrected her. "He'll be reading his poetry then."

Shanon gave Amy a sympathetic look. "I forgot all about that. What a bummer."

"I'm going to miss him all right." Amy nodded. "But I'm going to try to go to the rehearsal of his reading—the day before the real thing. I'm sure Miss Gray—"

"Oh, no!" Shanon interrupted her. "I just thought of something awful."

"What is it?" Amy asked anxiously.

Shanon gave her a stricken look. "If Miss Grayson marries Mr. Griffith, that means we're not only going to lose him, we're going to lose her also!"

Amy puckered her lips thoughtfully. "How do you get that?" she asked.

Shanon shrugged. "It's a given. Mr. Griffith will be her

husband. She'll want to go where he goes. She'll probably get a job teaching in the same school he does."

"Maybe she won't," said Amy. "Maybe Mr. Griffith will find a job teaching close by so he can travel back and forth every day."

"He was looking for a job in Princeton," Shanon reminded her. "That's not exactly within commuting distance."

Lisa slurped her shake. "Well, it's definitely a bummer. I wish she wouldn't go."

"I still say she doesn't have to," Amy insisted.

"Come on," Lisa said, "that's the way it works when people are engaged or married. My mom goes wherever my dad's business takes him. She even goes along on his business trips."

"Not my mother," said Amy. "She's a photo journalist. She travels around a lot, just like my dad does. Sometimes they're in different cities—or even countries—for months at a time!"

"How awful," said Shanon. "They must really miss each other. I don't think my mom and dad have spent a night apart since they got married. They have it all worked out. My dad takes care of the garage, and my mom runs the house."

Palmer laughed uneasily. "My parents have worked things out, too. They never do *anything* together."

"That's because they're divorced," Amy said gently. "But what about when they *did* live together?"

Palmer shrugged. "Dad went to the office. Mom gave parties. What can I say?"

"Well, when *I* get married," Amy said firmly, "nobody's going to tell me where to live, even if he is my husband."

Lisa laughed. "That's a long time from now."

"So what?" Amy said. "I can still have an opinion about it. I wouldn't even mind if I did all the work outside of the house and my husband stayed home and did the housework."

"Oh, no!" Palmer shrieked. "You don't want one of those Mr. Mom types!"

"I wouldn't laugh," Shanon chimed in. "It's very modern. I bet if Mars lived with a girl, he wouldn't mind doing dishes and that kind of stuff."

"Oh, my gosh!" gasped Lisa. "Can you imagine what Mars Martinez would say if he knew you had called him a Mr. Mom type?"

Shanon's face turned red. "I did not call him that! So please don't pass it around. I just think it's nice to keep an open mind. Every generation has its own way of doing things. Maybe by the time we're in our twenties, marriage will be a lot different than it is nowadays."

As Amy turned up her glass to get the last dregs of her choc-shot, Lisa pulled away from the table. "I've got a great idea," she giggled.

"What?" Amy asked with a smile.

Lisa leaned back in conspiratorially. "Wouldn't it be fun if we sent questionnaires to our pen pals and got their opinions on these kinds of things?"

"*We* have opinions," Palmer agreed. "*They* probably do, too!"

"I bet theirs are very old-fashioned," said Amy.

"This is a way to find out!" said Shanon. "I have a boy cousin who once told me that a girl could never be President."

"That's a real caveman mentality," said Amy. "In other

countries there are women leaders who do great jobs."

"I don't know about that," Palmer said hesitantly. "I'm not sure I'd have the dedication to be President. There probably wouldn't be any time for shopping."

The other Foxes groaned.

"When are we going to think up the questions?" Amy asked eagerly. "We should make them really funny."

"Maybe tonight," Lisa said, glancing at her watch. "Right now, Amy and I have rehearsal." And with that, they both got up from the table.

"Good luck, you two," Shanon said. "If Gina asks about the costumes, tell her I'm working on them."

"I'm going to help!" Palmer said generously.

Shanon turned to Palmer as their suitemates hurried out of the snack bar. "Looks like those two are getting along better," she said happily.

"They can't stay mad at each other for long," said Palmer.

Shanon leaned on her elbow. "I hope nothing happens at the rehearsal this afternoon. The Ardies are going to be at this one."

"Oh, they'll be fine," Palmer said, jumping up from the table. "We've got more important things to worry about now. Let's go! I want to get started!"

"On the costumes?" said Shanon.

"No, on our questionnaire! I've got the perfect title for it!"

Shanon chuckled. "Let's hear it!"

Palmer spread out her arms dramatically. "Caveman or Modern—Which Will You Be in Seven Years?"

CHAPTER THIRTEEN

Lisa stopped just outside the theater and put her hand on Amy's arm. "I have something to tell you before we go in," she said awkwardly.

Amy stared at her. "If it's about this thing with the kiss. . . ."

"It is, sort of," Lisa confessed. "I just want you to know I didn't mean all that stuff I said the other day."

"I was pretty hard on you, too," Amy admitted. "It must have been rough losing the female lead like that with Rob playing the male lead."

"Thanks for understanding," Lisa said gratefully. "Jealousy is a weird emotion. It makes you say and do awful things."

Amy gave her a playful punch on the shoulder. "You don't have anything to worry about. I've got enough on my mind with all the songs I have to learn and getting to John's poetry reading rehearsal."

"Hey, Foxes!"

Lisa whirled around at the sound of Rob's familiar voice, and her heart started thumping immediately. *This time I'm not going to act dumb,* she told herself.

"How are you, Everyman?" Amy said teasingly.

"Great," Rob replied, putting an arm around each of the girls' shoulders. "Just going a little crazy with all these women around," he joked. "Twice on the Alma campus in two weeks is strong medicine."

Lisa chuckled uneasily. She liked the fact that he had his arm on her shoulder—but she couldn't help wishing he didn't have his other arm on Amy's.

But Amy was already moving gracefully away from Rob. "I'm going in to run over some lines," she excused herself with a smile.

Lisa smiled back at her. It was nice of Amy to leave her alone with Rob for a moment.

"Hey!" Rob took his arm off Lisa's shoulder. "Don't go, Everywoman . . . ha, ha, I mean, Amy."

Lisa frowned. Rob was really carrying this play thing too far!

"What is it?" Amy asked matter-of-factly.

Rob blushed. "I, uh, wanted to discuss the . . . you know. . . ." He glanced uneasily at Lisa, who got the distinct impression that Rob wanted her to get lost.

"If you have something private to say . . ." Lisa began.

"There's nothing we have to talk about that you can't hear," Amy jumped in.

Rob frowned. "No, of course not. I just thought it might bore Lisa. It's about Everyman and Everywoman. You know—the *big* moment." He chuckled again, this time looking even more embarrassed.

Lisa lifted an eyebrow. She was starting to get jealous all

over again. "What *big moment* is that?" she asked peevishly. As if she didn't know!

"You mean the kiss?" Amy said, glancing at Rob. "I can't understand it myself." She shrugged. "But I guess Gina will explain everything the day we rehearse it."

"I'd like to be there for that," Lisa said sarcastically.

Just then Gina walked up. "Hey, stars!" she called out, greeting Amy and Rob. Then she smiled at Lisa. "Hi there, Beauty."

"What is this?" Lisa said irritably. "We're still ourselves, aren't we? Just because I'm playing the part of Beauty doesn't mean I've turned into her." What she really wanted to say was just because Rob's and Amy's *characters* are supposed to be in love, that doesn't mean *they* have to be—but she didn't.

"Sorry," Gina said thoughtfully. "You're right. When you're doing a play, it's important to keep a handle on your own identity. My dad told me about that. He's a professional actor. He once played a sick person and got so into the part that one day at rehearsal he actually started feeling sick himself."

"Heavy," said Amy.

"He got lost in his role?" Lisa asked curiously.

"I guess he did for a little while," Gina answered. "I sure don't recommend it."

"Oh, I don't know," Rob said. "Everyman's such a cool role, I wouldn't mind getting lost in it for a while. In fact, I wouldn't mind being a real actor."

Oh, brother! thought Lisa. *Next thing he'll be saying is that he wants to get lost in Amy's kiss!*

"By the way," Rob said to Gina. "I wanted to talk to you about something."

95

Gina turned to him. "What?"

Rob's face flushed. "My, uh, *favorite* part," he chuckled.

"He's talking about the kiss," Amy volunteered.

"What about it?" Gina asked Rob.

"Well, I, uh, I was just wondering. . . ."

"Don't you like that part?" Gina asked with a serious expression. "I thought about it a long time. I knew I was taking a chance putting in something like that."

"Yes, it's a bold move," Rob admitted, "and I really do like the kiss. I really do! But . . ." He glanced at Amy and then at Lisa and let out a sigh. "Forget it," he told Gina. "I'll talk to you later."

"Fine," Gina said. "After rehearsal. But now let's go inside. I want to run through that first scene between Everyman and Everywoman." She glanced back at Lisa. "You can wait here if you want, Beauty—oops, I mean Lisa! I won't be needing you for a while."

"Sure," Lisa said, her heart sinking as she watched Amy and Rob disappear through the doors with Gina. Then she gave her head a little shake. It was a beautiful day—why shouldn't she wait on the steps instead of indoors? Maybe she could chat with some of the other cast members—some of the other Ardies! But instead of joining into a conversation, Lisa found a corner and sat by herself.

I don't believe this! she thought unhappily. All along, she'd assumed that Amy was the one who liked Rob, but now it seemed very clear that it was Rob who liked Amy! Hadn't he put his arm around her shoulder? Hadn't he just about admitted he'd lost his own identity in the role of Everyman? And the kiss was his favorite part of the whole play! He'd said so! He couldn't wait to discuss it with the director—privately!

He probably wants her to put another *kiss in,* Lisa thought. She tossed her long, dark hair and sighed. She'd even worn Rob's class pin today. It was right on her collar. But Rob hadn't even noticed. He probably wished he'd never given it to her in the first place, she thought.

With another big sigh, Lisa stood up and glanced around. Practically the whole chorus was standing outside. People were talking and joking with each other as if they were at a party. Brenda Smith and Kate were even eating ice-cream cones. And Muffin was flirting with a cute Ardie! Everyone seemed to be having a great time. Everyone but her!

CHAPTER FOURTEEN

———◆———

ARE YOU A CAVEMAN OR MODERN?
ANSWER THESE SIMPLE QUESTIONS AND FIND OUT!
RETURN TO: SHANON DAVIS, AMY HO, PALMER DURAND, AND
LISA MCGREEVY (THE FOXES OF THE THIRD DIMENSION!)

1. If a boy and girl are roommates, which one of them do you think should do the dishes?
2. If a girl and boy go out to the movies, which one should pay for the tickets?
3. If a girl and a boy who are in love graduate from college and each gets a job in a different city, which city should they move to—the one where the boy's job is or the one where the girl's job is?
4. If a girl is taller than a boy, do you think it is okay to still have her as a girlfriend?
5. If a girl and a boy have a fight, which one should be the first to apologize?

"These are hard questions," said Palmer, chewing the end of her pencil. "I thought our questionnaire was going to be funny. You're making it sound too serious."

"I think it's more interesting this way," Shanon replied.

"Okay, I've got another one!" Shanon said excitedly. "If you were on an all-boys' team and a girl who was an excellent athlete wanted to try out for it, how would you feel?"

"That *is* a good one," Palmer agreed, "but what's the right answer?"

Shanon walked back to the sewing machine. "That you should welcome the girl on the team, of course," she said, starting to stitch a new seam. The costume she was working on was for Lisa. "Any guy who doesn't think women can be good athletes is definitely a caveman."

Palmer picked up one of the mini-skirts and began hemming it. "What about the other questions, though? We'd better discuss them ourselves first. Otherwise we won't know how to score the guys when we get their answers back."

"Good idea," Shanon mumbled, holding a straight pin in her mouth. She continued sewing until Lisa walked into the suite an hour later.

"Just in time to try on your costume!" Shanon said, stopping the sewing machine and lifting up the full, colorful skirt.

"It's nice," Lisa said quietly.

"It is an unusual design," Shanon admitted, "but it's what Gina wanted. Why don't you try it on now?"

"Okay," Lisa said, unenthusiastically slipping the skirt on over her jeans.

"Wow," said Palmer. "You look great. Wait until you have your leggings and leotard on."

Even Lisa had to admit it was cute. "Are you going to finish the rest of the costumes in time?" she asked Shanon, glancing around the cluttered sitting room.

"Kate and some other girls are coming by this evening to help," Shanon said, laying out another pattern.

"We're going to have a sewing bee!" Palmer announced as Lisa got out of the skirt and headed for her room.

"Where's Amy?" Shanon called after her. "Still at rehearsal?"

"Gina asked her and Rob to stay late," Lisa said flatly. "Another private rehearsal."

"Don't go into your room," said Palmer, jumping up. "You haven't read the questionnaire yet." She shoved the piece of paper into Lisa's hand.

"I'll read it in my room," Lisa said, barely looking at it. "Now, if you'll excuse me, I'd like some privacy."

"Looks like things didn't go so well at the rehearsal," Shanon surmised as the bedroom door closed quietly behind Lisa.

"Maybe the questionnaire will cheer her up," said Palmer.

But Lisa wasn't at all interested in the latest Fox Project. Stretched out on her bed, she let the questionnaire fall to the floor, then rolled over onto her stomach and reached for a notebook. The rehearsal ended just the way it started, with Amy and Rob together. It seemed to Lisa that Gina hardly paid attention to the big scene between Beauty and Everyman. And Rob had been so busy trying to remember his lines that he'd never once looked Lisa in the eye.

Lisa's hand searched the floor for a pen. After a moment of painful thought, she began to write:

Dear Rob,
Enclosed is your class pin. . . .

100

CHAPTER FIFTEEN

———————⬥———————

Dear Rob, John, and Mars:
    Please fill out the latest Fox Questionnaire and send your answers to us. As you can tell, we are interested in some very serious questions. We'd like your opinions for the sake of discussion.

Yours truly,
Foxes of the Third Dimension

Dear Sam,
    Would you mind filling out this questionnaire? We are interested in knowing what boys today think. Amy, Lisa, and Shanon are also sending one of these to each of their pen pals at Ardsley. I have another question for you now—how would you like to come to our school play next Sunday afternoon? Both Lisa and Amy are in it. And I will be there in the audience. I hope you can come!

Sincerely,
Palmer

Dear Foxes,
    Sorry, but your questionnaire is too heavy. We cannot

answer it on the grounds that it may incriminate us. In other words, we plead the Fifth Amendment. We also are of the opinion that these issues are baloney to discuss at our age.

John Adams, Mars Martinez, Rob Williams
P.S. If a girl was good enough, we all agree that she should be on a boys' sports team, especially if she has a good personality and a good throwing arm!

Dear Palmer,

Thank you for the invitation to the play. I will definitely be there! Your questionnaire is clever and has some good questions. Here are my answers. Please let me know what you think about all this.

1. The boy and girl should get a dishwasher.
2. The boy and girl going to the movies should flip a coin to see who treats.
3. The boy and girl getting jobs in two different cities should pick a third city halfway in between and each try to find a job there.
4. You cannot base whether you like a girl or not on height because boys and girls are still growing. You might start out liking a short girl and she could turn out to be taller than you someday. Then what would you do?
5. If two people have a fight, the one who knows he is the less stubborn should apologize first. Some people find it too hard to apologize.
6. Girls should be allowed to be on boys' teams if they are tough enough.

"Sam's answers sound really modern," Palmer said proudly.

"I agree," said Shanon.

"At least he didn't cop out like our pen pals did," said Amy.

The three girls were in the big third-floor bathroom, washing up together.

Amy tousled her hair in the mirror, so it looked even spikier than usual. "Anybody seen Lisa? What does she think of the questionnaire?"

"Beats me," said Shanon. "I've hardly seen her in days, and she's my roommate."

"She certainly hasn't been eating her meals with us," Palmer agreed, slathering pink moisturizer onto her flawless complexion.

"And whenever she comes into the suite, she shuts herself in our room," Shanon volunteered. "Half the time she doesn't even say goodnight to me."

Amy tossed a towel over her shoulder. "I hope she's not still jealous about my playing Everywoman or that kiss Rob and I have to do."

"I doubt it," said Shanon. "That would be pretty silly."

"All the same," said Amy, "I don't think I'd better tell her that Rob's coming with me to John's poetry reading rehearsal."

"How come he's doing that?" asked Palmer.

"Rob wants to see John do his thing just like I do. He'll be at Alma for an early rehearsal just before, so we're going to bike into town together. Why don't you two come with us?"

"Thanks," said Palmer, "but I only have one town pass left. I want to save it in case Sam asks me out again."

"I'd better not go either," Shanon said. "I'm sure I'll have lots of last-minute sewing to do that day. But wish John luck for me. And I think you're right not to mention the part about Rob to Lisa. She's so moody these days—especially when it comes to him!"

"I won't say anything to her about it either," said Palmer.

But as they left the bathroom and padded down the hall in their slippers, Shanon started having second thoughts. When she got back to her room, Lisa was already in bed with the lights out.

"Are you awake?" Shanon whispered.

Shanon had a feeling Lisa was still awake, but there was no answer.

Shanon sighed and pulled the covers over her head. Amy was probably right. Why get Lisa all upset over nothing?

CHAPTER SIXTEEN

———◆———

Lisa was doing her best to avoid everyone. She was too embarrassed to confide her true feelings—even to Shanon. She'd acted dumb enough a few weeks back when she'd accused Amy of wanting to kiss Rob. How could she admit that she was still feeling jealous? Or that she was so unhappy she was thinking about dropping Rob as her pen pal? Anyway, Shanon would probably just give her a pep talk and insist she had nothing to be jealous about!

But Lisa didn't need any pep talks. She *knew* Rob liked Amy. So the best thing to do was simply forget the fact that he was *her* friend to begin with. Of course she still thought Rob was a neat person. And she certainly still liked Amy. It would take a while, she thought glumly, but she'd just have to get used to it being the two of them together instead of her and Rob.

As she walked up the path to the theater, Lisa felt inside the pocket of her skirt. The letter with Rob's class pin was in a pink envelope. She hadn't wanted to send it in the mail because it was too personal. So she'd decided to wait and deliver it to him in person after the dress rehearsal.

She paused in front of the double doors, reluctant to go inside. Today was the day Amy and Rob were supposed to practice the kiss. *I might as well get it over with,* she thought with a heavy heart.

"Hi, there!" Gina greeted Lisa at the door. Inside the theater, Lisa could see other members of the chorus and some of the cast from Ardsley already gathering.

"Hi," Lisa whispered.

"Are you okay?" Gina asked. "You look kind of green."

"I'm okay," Lisa said dully. How could she explain that she was green with jealousy?

Gina took her hand. "I'm glad you're here. I wanted to tell you what a good job you're doing."

Lisa looked surprised. "Really? Thanks."

"No, thank *you*," Gina said, smiling. "To be honest, I've really been winging it here. This is the first play I ever wrote in my life, and I'm pretty nervous."

"You don't seem to be," Lisa observed.

"Looks can be deceiving," said Gina. "There are a couple of things I wish I'd done differently."

"What?" Lisa asked curiously.

"Some of the words are kind of intellectual," Gina said with a worried frown. "And I think maybe I made the costumes too complicated. Shanon has worked so hard on them!"

"I think she enjoyed doing it though," Lisa said kindly.

"Oh, well," Gina quipped, "I can always change them when the play goes to Broadway!"

Lisa laughed as she walked down the aisle with Gina. For a moment she'd forgotten all about Rob. She gazed up on the stage at the freshly painted set. It looked great, almost professional. Things were really taking shape with the play, and the whole theater seemed suddenly alive with excitement. Downstage by the stairs, she saw Shanon helping Brenda Smith try on her costume.

"Whether they were hard work or not," Lisa assured Gina, "the costumes are fabulous. I love mine."

"I can't wait to see you in it," Gina said. "I told Shanon to make sure it stood out."

"You did?" Lisa asked.

"Sure," said Gina. "Your role isn't that big, but it's very important. In fact, it's my favorite in the play."

Lisa gulped. "It is?"

"You represent the beauty and nobility present in all mankind," Gina explained. "From the moment you said you wanted to try out for the play, I had you in mind for Beauty."

"Wow," said Lisa, flattered. "I hope I do a good job."

Gina shrugged. "Like I said, you're perfect. In fact, I'm starting today with your monologue. See you later—I've got to talk with Kate," she said and hopped onto the stage.

Climbing onto the stage as well, Lisa tapped Gina on the shoulder. "Excuse me," she said, "I don't understand . . ."

Gina turned back. "Yes?"

"You said we're starting with my monologue?" said Lisa. "That's in the middle of the play. I thought this was supposed to be a complete dress rehearsal."

"It was," Gina told her. "But Amy and Rob had to leave early."

"Why? Where did they go?" Lisa asked in confusion.

"They went into town," Gina explained. "Amy asked me about it a few days ago. She said something about a poetry reading. It sounded important, so I scheduled a separate rehearsal for her and Rob this morning. We can put the whole play together tomorrow in tech rehearsal."

Lisa's stomach began to churn. Things between Amy and Rob were obviously even more serious than she'd imagined. They were out on a *date* together!

Gina stepped aside to speak with Kate, but Lisa remained in the middle of the stage, staring into space. People hustled back and forth with pieces of the set. Up above, a girl on a ladder was checking the lights. Other members of the chorus paraded by in their costumes while Bob Brown ran through some of the songs on the piano. Mr. Griffith entered the theater and took a seat in the back.

Suddenly Lisa felt someone shaking her shoulder. It was Gina.

"Hey," the director laughed, "you're a thousand miles away. Mind if I hear your monologue now?"

"Now?" Lisa gasped, looking around in confusion. Most of the cast had gone backstage. The freshly painted back-drops were in place, drying. Even the girl with the ladder was nowhere to be seen.

"Sorry, I must have been daydreaming," Lisa said. "I should have gotten into costume like everyone else."

"You can do that in a minute," Gina assured her. "There's something in the monologue I want to point out to you first."

"You look great in that light, Lisa!" Mr. Griffith called from his seat in the audience as Gina walked back to confer with him for a moment.

Lisa blinked. The stage lights were on. "Are you sure you want me to do it now?" she asked Gina.

"Yes, just as you are," Gina replied, taking a seat. The theater was very quiet. Lisa stepped forward.

"I am Beauty," she said. "Touch me. Those who come to

108

know me, live forever. Like a dark and crystal well, I am deep. I—"

"Hold it!" Gina interrupted. "That's the spot. I get the feeling you don't understand what that means."

Lisa's face flushed. "I guess I don't," she confessed. "When I think of a well, I think of water, not a person."

"Try thinking of a deep pool of fresh water that goes on forever," Gina suggested. "A place inside yourself where you can go when times are rough and come back feeling renewed."

Tears sprang to Lisa's eyes. Something in Gina's words had touched her. She stepped forward again and spoke out. Now her voice was clear and strong with emotion.

"Like a dark and crystal well, I am deep. I am Beauty. Come and know me!"

CHAPTER SEVENTEEN

The next day was the technical rehearsal, and this time the entire cast was present—including Rob and Amy. Just before rehearsal started, Lisa slipped into the boys' dressing room and found Rob's spot at the table. She tucked the pink envelope under his script. It had taken her hours to write the short note, but she thought it was a good one.

Dear Rob,

Enclosed is your class pin. I get the feeling that we are both too young to think of ourselves as boyfriend and girlfriend. I have had this feeling a lot since the play started. So I hope you don't mind my giving the pin back to you. You are a nice person. I know that, in spite of everything.

Yours,
Lisa

Lisa stared at the envelope with tears in her eyes. What else could she say? She just hoped Rob would wait a little while before giving the pin to Amy.

"You're wanted on stage," Shanon called, passing by quickly.

"Okay," Lisa replied. "I'm coming." She hurried to catch up with her roommate. "Did you finish the last costume?"

Shanon tried to smile and yawn at the same time. She had stayed up almost the whole night, sewing with her assistants. Miss Grayson had given them special permission. "All done," she reported. "I'm especially proud of the one I made for you."

Lisa flushed. "Thanks for doing such a good job on it."

Shanon touched her hand. "Are you mad at me or something?"

"No," Lisa said, surprised.

"I just wondered," said Shanon. "You haven't said a word to me in days."

"Sorry. I've had something on my mind," Lisa confessed.

"I've had something on my mind, too," Shanon said. "Mars can't come to the play tomorrow afternoon. John Adams is having his poetry reading at the same time. Mars had to flip a coin to decide which one of his roommates' events he was going to see—John's or Rob's. It turns out he's going to the poetry reading."

"That's too bad," said Lisa. "I had forgotten all about it until I heard that Amy went to John's rehearsal yesterday."

"She said he was great," Shanon said brightly.

Lisa lowered her eyes. "Did you know that she and Rob went together?" she asked softly.

Shanon squeezed her hand. "I know. We didn't want to tell you because—"

"You don't have to explain," Lisa said, blinking a tear back. "I've given up being jealous."

"But you shouldn't be," Shanon began. "There's nothing—"

"All actors onstage!" Kate yelled, peering backstage. "The director wants a word with the cast before we begin!"

"I'd better go," Lisa said. She squeezed Shanon's hand in return. "Thanks for being my friend. I'll explain everything later."

While Shanon turned back to the girls' dressing room, Lisa headed for the stage. The entire cast was huddled on the set, and Lisa slipped in next to Brenda. Rob was on the other side of the stage, standing with Amy. He caught Lisa's eye and waved to her. Lisa gulped and waved back. She had promised herself to be as friendly as she could to him and Amy. She had also decided to forget about them for an hour or so and focus as hard as she could on the play. That part shouldn't be too difficult, not after the exciting rehearsal she'd had with Gina the day before. In the past few weeks, she'd been so busy thinking about Rob that she'd paid very little attention to her role in the play. Now she was determined to make the most of the time she had left to work on Beauty.

"I want to thank you all!" Gina was telling the cast. "This has been a great experience, and you're the ones who've made it that. Today's rehearsal is going to take a lot of concentration. We'll be walking through several scenes to make sure the lights are set properly. And I'll want to hear some of the songs we've been having problems with. Then, this afternoon, we'll put everything together and run it through nonstop!"

"Oh, no," Brenda moaned. "Suppose one of us forgets something?"

"That might happen," Gina allowed, "but if you keep

112

your minds on what you're supposed to do next and where you're supposed to be, it probably won't.

"Now, I'm going to ask you all to remain either backstage or in the audience area whenever you're not onstage," she went on. "And there shouldn't be any talking, please. It'll spoil the concentration for everyone else."

"Do you want to run through the sound cues?" Kate asked, approaching Gina.

"Okay," Gina said with a nod, "and let's check on the levels. Amy and Rob!—I'd like to hear a couple of your solo numbers with the guitar and microphones. Then I'll hear Brenda, Larry, and Muffin. The rest of you can relax for a while."

Lisa slipped backstage and through one of the doors that led to the audience. From the back of the auditorium, she watched Gina and the other actors work through scene after scene. She listened to Amy and Rob singing. She witnessed the magic of the lights and admired the set. And when it came time for her one song and her scene with Rob, she went up and gave it her all.

"Great play, isn't it?" Rob whispered, catching her backstage.

As Lisa glanced at him in confusion, Rob gave her one of his great grins.

"Did you, uh, get my letter?" she asked quietly.

Rob grinned. "Yep. I have it in my pocket."

Lisa gulped. "Uh, good. Maybe you'd better wait till you're back in school to read it though."

"Why?" Rob whispered, grinning again. "Something personal in it?"

Lisa backed away awkwardly. "I . . . I'm going to wait for my cue over here," she mumbled uncomfortably.

Kate threw them a sharp glance. "Shhh! No talking back-stage! Remember?"

Lisa found a corner in the wings to stand in. Onstage she could see Amy doing a scene with Brenda and one of the boys. She glanced back over her shoulder. Rob was still standing in the same spot, but now he was staring at her with a hurt expression on his face. He had opened the pink envelope and crumpled it in his hand. Lisa felt her own hands turn to ice. Tearing her eyes away from Rob, she looked at the stage and tried to clear her mind of everything but *Everypeople*.

The afternoon of the performance, the theater was buzz-ing. Before the audience arrived, the performers dashed to and fro, wishing each other good luck and getting into their costumes. Kate and the other stage manager made hurried last-minute adjustments on the set. The boys and girls run-ning the lights and sound equipment checked their cues one more time. Mr. Griffith and Miss Grayson arrived to help out with the final details.

Gina and Bob Brown stood nervously at the door to the theater. Gina was wearing a corsage of little pink roses that the girls in the cast had given her.

"Anything we can do?" Mr. Griffith asked Gina. "Not that I've done anything during the rehearsals but sit around and look like a teacher."

"We could pass out programs," Miss Grayson volun-teered cheerfully.

Gina pointed to the crew of ushers standing near the doorway. "We've got some students to do that."

"Looks like you kids have everything under control," Mr. Griffith said.

"All but one thing," Gina said, smiling. "Our nerves! I'm not even going to be out there and I have a terrible case of stage fright! I can imagine how the performers feel!"

Backstage, Amy paced nervously. Her sleek leggings and short skirt were offset by a black leotard, and her shiny dark hair was slicked back dramatically. On the outside, she was all composure. But inside, her stomach was doing flip-flops. She had eight songs in the play! She didn't know whether she wanted to jump right onstage that very moment and get the whole thing over with, or peel off her costume and slink back to the dorm. She'd never been so scared—or excited—in her life. She was thrilled to be a part of something so many other people had cared so much about. She only wished her pen pal could be there. . . .

Meanwhile, Lisa was feeling just as nervous as Amy—and just as excited. She stared at herself in the dressing-room mirror as she applied her mascara with shaking hands. Her face glowed with anticipation, and her eyes shone brightly. Even her hair looked glossier than usual. For one magical instant, she knew she looked truly like Beauty!

On her table was a vase with a big shasta daisy from Amy and a white peony from Shanon and Palmer with a note attached that said "Break a leg!" Lisa touched the two flowers lovingly. Next to them was a pink rose. It had been left with no note on her table. Lisa noticed that Amy had one, too.

Shanon took her seat in the audience, and glanced eagerly around her. The theater was filling up rapidly. The air seemed filled with expectancy—as if something remarkable was about to happen any minute. She sat back in her chair and relaxed. Two aisles down she saw Miss Grayson and Mr. Griffith, but they only saw each other. Then Miss Pryn came in with some other faculty members. Instead of the stern expression she usually wore, the headmistress was smiling radiantly. Shanon looked up at the stage for a minute. Soon she would see her costumes under the lights. The work had been incredibly hard, and she was exhausted. But she knew her efforts had all been worth it.

Palmer waited anxiously in the lobby. In just five minutes the curtain would go up, and Sam still hadn't come. *Maybe he forgot,* she thought desperately. But then a tall, handsome boy with shaggy blond hair strolled into the theater. "I hope I'm not late," he said, smiling.

"Sam!" exclaimed Palmer, running across the lobby to meet him. She looked into his eyes and suddenly found herself tongue-tied. "I—I haven't seen you in a long time," she finally managed.

"Likewise," Sam said, flushing as he presented her with a bag from behind his back. "I brought you something."

"A present!" Palmer cried. She plunged her hand into the shopping bag and came up with a dark blue T-shirt. A splash of golden stars was painted across the front.

"It's beautiful," said Palmer.

"My sister made it," Sam said. "I, uh, asked her to. Recognize the constellation?"

"It's the Big Dipper!"

Sam grinned. "It was part of the plan—you know, my special surprise. That's why I asked you your favorite colors and stars."

"Wow," said Palmer, "that's really nice of you."

Sam blushed. "I also brought you a tape of me and The Fantasy since you like our music. Sorry about the banana split with pistachio ice cream. Maybe next time."

"That's okay," Palmer said, clutching her new T-shirt.

Sam took Palmer's hand. "I guess we'd better go in now. . . ."

A hush fell over the audience as the houselights went down and the stage lights came up. The first chord of Gina's original music sounded on the electric guitar, followed by a rollicking hard-rock piano overture banged out by Bob Brown. The curtain slowly rose, and Everyman and Everywoman stepped out onto the stage, followed closely by Soul. Beauty, Heart, Riches, and the rest of the cast waited tensely in the wings to make their entrances. There was no more time for last-minute problems or even nervousness as the magic of the theater swept them all up. The actors and the audience were transported. And the play began!

CHAPTER EIGHTEEN

"Bravo! Bravo!" Mr. Griffith's deep voice boomed out from the audience. The crowd clapped loudly as the actors took their bows, then joined hands and sang an encore of the title song . . . "Everypeople." The two leads, Amy and Rob, stepped forward and bowed to each other. Then Gina and Bob were brought up onstage and the whole company bowed together again. The audience's applause thundered in their ears.

"You were great!" Shanon cried, catching Lisa backstage just after the curtain came down. "The whole thing was incredible. My eyes were glued to the stage! And the music! . . ."

"Wasn't it fantastic!" Lisa exclaimed as Amy dashed up to them.

"Amy!" cried Shanon.

"Hi!" she squealed. "Did you like it?"

Shanon hugged her. "I *loved* it!"

Rob came up behind Lisa. "You were really good." He grinned, breathing down her neck.

Lisa blushed and turned toward him. "So . . . so were you," she stammered. "I'm sorry I didn't see every scene."

"The one we had together was my favorite," Rob said earnestly.

Lisa blinked. "Really?"

He looked into her eyes. "Really."

Lisa held his gaze and smiled, but she didn't know what to say. She and Rob hadn't spoken since he read her letter.

"I think I know why you wrote me that letter," Rob finally said. "It's because of that questionnaire you sent that I refused to fill out. But I can still fill it out if you want me to."

"Questionnaire?" squeaked Lisa.

"Wasn't Lisa great?" Amy bubbled, throwing her arms around her suitemate. "She was a perfect Beauty!"

Rob smiled. "I was just telling her that."

"How did you like the way Rob and I fixed up the kiss?" Amy giggled into Lisa's ear.

"The kiss?" Lisa choked. It was the one scene she'd purposely avoided watching. Luckily, Beauty didn't have to be onstage for it. Even in the technical rehearsal the day before, Lisa'd headed for the dressing room when she knew it was coming up. "What about the kiss?" Lisa asked faintly. "I'm afraid I missed that part."

"It was a great moment," Shanon enthused. "Whoever thought of changing the kiss to a big hug was right on."

Amy smiled. "It was Rob's idea. But I must say I agreed. I always thought the kiss was too romantic."

"Wait a minute!" Lisa exclaimed. "Are you telling me you took the kiss out?"

Rob nodded. "I never wanted it in. It took me a while to work up the courage to ask Gina about it. And then," he added shyly, "I was kind of afraid of insulting Amy."

"Believe me," said Amy, "I wasn't insulted—I was relieved. That kiss was so-o-o-o corny!"

"But you said it was your favorite part," Lisa blurted out, turning to Rob.

Rob looked puzzled. "I must have been making a joke—you know, being sarcastic," he said with a shrug.

Amy glanced around excitedly. Backstage the cast and crew were all in a flurry. Most of the actors were already out of their costumes. "Coming to the cast party?" she asked Lisa and Rob.

Rob grabbed Lisa's arm. "Wouldn't miss it."

"I hear they're actually having ice cream and stuff so people can make their own banana splits and sundaes," Shanon said excitedly. "Palmer and Sam are already on their way over! I wish Mars could be here."

Rob laughed. "Right! Then he could really make himself into a piggie!"

"I wish John were here, too," Amy said wistfully.

Amy gave Lisa another big bear hug. Then she hugged Rob, too. "You were a great leading man," she said, her eyes sparkling with joy. "This has been a perfect day. I'll never forget it."

"Neither will I," Rob said.

Lisa stood back as Rob returned Amy's hug. But this time, for some reason, she didn't feel jealous at all!

Amy beamed at Lisa, and then she and Shanon dashed off toward the dressing room. "See you later!" Shanon cried.

And suddenly Lisa and Rob were alone in the wings.

"About that letter I wrote," Lisa said shyly.

"I'll fill out the questionnaire," Rob said, shuffling his feet. "You, uh, don't have to wear the pin if you don't want to, though."

"Oh, but I *want* to wear it!" Lisa cried. "I mean . . ." she added quietly, "it was childish of me to give it back."

Rob smiled. "I know how touchy you girls are about those Fox things," he said, "but I had no idea you'd get so mad when I pleaded the Fifth." He stared at Lisa. "That *is* the reason you got mad at me, isn't it?"

"What else *could* it have been?" Lisa said helplessly. She wanted to tell Rob how jealous she'd been, but now it all seemed so silly. And this day was so special, she didn't want to ruin it. Maybe some other time she'd tell him just how dumb she'd been.

Suddenly Rob pulled her behind the stage curtain and kissed her.

"Wow!" Lisa murmured.

"Yeah, wow," Rob said softly. "I've been wanting to do that for a long time. You might say I've been rehearsing it—in my mind that is!"

Lisa giggled. "It was . . . a definite hit," she said.

Rob blushed. "Thanks. Did you get the flower I left for you?"

"The pink rose?" Lisa said in surprise.

Rob smiled. "Sure. John asked me to leave one for Amy also. When you didn't throw yours away, I figured you couldn't be all that mad at me."

"I'm not mad anymore," said Lisa. Her face flushed. "And I never should have been in the first place. But I thought you and Amy went out on a date," she confessed all in a rush.

"A date?" said Rob. "You mean when we both went to see John's rehearsal? You should have been there. He was *great*! I hope the poetry reading went just as well today."

Lisa sighed. So much for Rob and Amy's big "date"! Now

121

that she thought of it, why shouldn't they have gone to see John together? They were friends, just like she and Amy were. Jealousy had made her forget that.

"Look around," Rob chuckled softly. "We're the last ones here." While she and Rob had been talking, everyone had left for the cast party. Hand in hand, they walked onto the stage. The lights were dim and all the seats in the audience were empty.

"Seems like a dream," Rob said. "Just a little while ago this place was jumping, and now. . . ."

"It *was* over pretty fast," Lisa agreed wistfully. She looked into Rob's eyes and blushed. "I guess we'd better get along, or there won't be any ice cream left for our banana splits."

CHAPTER NINETEEN

You are invited to a *SECRET* Wedding Shower for Miss Maggie Grayson, in Fox Common Room. This Thursday at 4:00!

Remember: It's a Secret!!!

R S V P

Amy Ho Shanon Davis Lisa McGreevy Palmer Durand

Lisa, Shanon, and Amy beamed as Palmer brought out the big cake with pink candied roses they'd helped make in Mrs. Butter's kitchen. The rest of the dorm were all gathered in the Common Room. There were even some guests who didn't live in Fox Hall, like Dolores Countee and Gina.

Miss Grayson laughed softly and wiped a tear away. "I'm really touched," she said. "You girls are wonderful!"

"Let's cut the cake!" cried Muffin Talbot.

"I'll dish out the ice cream," Gina volunteered.

"No, I'll do it," Dolores said, taking over. "You pass out the punch cups."

Shanon stood back and watched. She had a few tears of joy in her own eyes. The shower had been her idea, and everybody had shown up to make it perfect: Kate, Gina, Dolores, Germaine, Muffin, Dawn, Brenda—and, of course, the Foxes!

"This cake is fabulous!" Miss Grayson exclaimed, licking some icing off the tip of one finger. The diamond ring from Mr. Griffith sparkled brightly.

"Hey, save me one of the roses!" Lisa called out to Muffin, who was cutting the cake. "Pink's my favorite color now!"

"That's ever since Rob gave her a pink rose last week!" Amy quipped loudly, and the room filled with laughter. Everyone quieted down as Miss Grayson settled on the couch to open her gift. "You girls are naughty," she scolded with a twinkle in her eye. "You shouldn't spend money on your teachers."

"We all chipped in for it," Dolores assured her.

Miss Grayson carefully removed the silver paper and white bow from the large square package. Inside, the gift was covered with delicate layers of tissue paper. "It must be something fragile," she said questioningly.

The girls giggled softly. No one was going to tell. They waited in hushed anticipation for their teacher to uncover her gift.

"It's beautiful!" she gasped, holding up an exquisite cut-glass pitcher.

"Dolores picked it out," Kate volunteered. "She got it at an antique shop."

"I think it'll look great in your new house," said Brenda. "You and Mr. Griffith can use it at parties."

Miss Grayson beamed as she put the pitcher down gently. "Thank you, girls. I hope we'll be able to have all of you at one of those parties. But now," she added, rising to her feet, "let's enjoy *this* party!"

"Wait!" Lisa said. "There's another present!"

"More?" said Miss Grayson. "This is too much!"

"Wait until you see what it is," Amy said with a giggle. "You may wish we hadn't given it to you."

"We made it ourselves," Shanon explained, pulling a long, rectangular box from under the punch table. "That is, Lisa, Amy, Palmer, and I did."

"Is it something that's going to jump out at me?" Miss Grayson teased, accepting the box.

Lisa laughed. "It's definitely not alive, but it *may* jump out at you—in a manner of speaking, that is."

"I'm not even going to try to guess," Miss Grayson said as she eagerly undid the big pink bow and lifted the top off the box.

"Why, it's . . . it's amazing!" she said.

"Take it out!" cried Lisa.

"Yes, let us see!" said Kate. "What is it?"

Taking one end gently, Miss Grayson pulled out the long trailing Fox quilt. The coverlet was a riot of textures and colors—full, soft, and wonderfully warm-looking.

"It's a quilt," Miss Grayson said, teary-eyed once more.

"It's our own design," Shanon said. She stepped forward to help the teacher hold it up.

"It looks like a jigsaw puzzle," Brenda said. "A really beautiful one!"

"It's a great design," agreed Kate. "Look how bright it is!"

"That's what I meant about it jumping out at you!" Lisa chuckled.

"I love the colors!" said Gina. "It's like an abstract painting!"

All the girls gathered around to admire the quilt.

"A lot of the patches are really special," Lisa explained eagerly. "We put in pieces of our favorite old clothes and, well . . . some other stuff." She touched the green piece from Rob's shirt with her finger.

"I love the one you've got your hand on," said Miss Grayson. "It's so soft-looking. And that shade of green is gorgeous."

"It's the heart of the quilt," Lisa said, blushing.

Shanon leaned over and pointed to a flowered patch near the center. "Recognize this, Miss Grayson?" she asked playfully.

Miss Grayson laughed. "It's my old flowered blouse! What rascals you four are!"

"And that orange stripe," Amy cried, "is Mr. Griffith's old necktie!"

"Oh, no!" squealed Brenda. "Look how loud it is!"

"My future husband," Miss Grayson said with a laugh, "stands out in any crowd!" After carefully refolding the quilt and putting it back in the box, she gave each of the girls a thank-you kiss.

"I guess she'll take it with her when she and Mr. Griffith leave Alma," Shanon whispered to Lisa as they drifted over to the punch table.

"At least she'll have something to remember us by," Lisa replied wistfully.

Then Amy and Palmer joined them, and the four friends stood in a huddle.

"I think the party's going great," Amy said happily.

"Miss Grayson loved the quilt," Palmer added.

Lisa lifted her punch glass. "While we're together, let's drink a toast," she said. She looked at Shanon, Amy, and Palmer with glowing eyes. The other three lifted their glasses.

"To us?" said Shanon.

"Who else?" Amy quipped with a grin.

"To the Foxes of the Third Dimension!" pronounced Palmer.

"May we always be friends!" Lisa chimed in.

The girls clinked their glasses and took a sip.

"Did I hear you four toasting over there?" Kate called from across the room.

"Let's all have a toast together!" Dolores cried. "To Miss Grayson!"

"Hear, hear!" said Kate.

"And to our school!" Miss Grayson put in proudly. "To Alma Stephens!"

The four Foxes joined the rest of the group. After Miss Grayson's toast, there was a moment of silence. Then all the girls in the room raised their glasses and drank to each other.

127

Leave It to Wanda:
An open letter from Headmistress Corinne Pryn
Dear Wanda,

First of all, let me say that I am an avid reader of your column, so it seems appropriate that before the close of the school year I should write you a letter. A few weeks back, you seemed to be very angry because you thought the administration was planning to fire someone you considered to be a very good teacher. I want to assure you that we have no such plans. We do not intend to fire any of our current, very fine faculty. However, we have taken under consideration your suggestion that the students have more input in evaluating their teachers. You are right, Wanda! The faculty does spend most of its time with the students. Therefore, I am asking the Board to institute a new policy, beginning next fall. Once a semester, students will be asked to fill out evaluation forms for each of their teachers. This will allow the faculty to learn firsthand just what it is you appreciate about their teaching methods and any problems you may be having with the course. It will also allow the administration to enter into closer communication with its student body.

As to your grievance regarding Alma Stephens's association with Brighton High School, I am giving this matter serious consideration. Once again, you are right. There has been a tradition here that some might view as snobbish, a view that was recently brought to my attention by the Student Council. In response to these complaints, we have decided to update our policy regarding social events. Next year we will schedule these events not only in cooperation with Ardsley, but with the Brighton public school as well.

Sincerely,
Corinne Pryn, Headmistress
Alma Stephens School for Girls

Dear Sam,

I had to send you a copy of this letter that Miss Pryn our headmistress had printed in The Ledger's *"Leave It to Wanda" column! Isn't it cool? It just goes to show that if you feel really strongly about something, and you're not afraid to express it, most of the time people will listen to you. So I guess we'll be getting together with your school some-time in the future—although I still don't think I could go anywhere out of state.*

Thank you again for my Big Dipper T-shirt. I wear it all the time. And thank you for coming to the play. Even though it wasn't what we originally had planned, to me it was a true dream date.

Write soon,
Palmer

Dear Palmer,

I'm glad you like the shirt. I can't wait until Brighton has some joint events with Alma. How about a talent show or a track-and-field day?

Write soon,
Sam

Dear Shanon, Lisa, Amy, and Palmer,

Dan and I want to thank you for the wonderful home-made quilt! We will always cherish it. I also appreciated the great shower you gave me. Dan and I thought you might like to know where we will be next year—right here at Alma Stephens!

Dan has decided to stay on for a while, and Miss Pryn has kindly offered us a lovely, larger apartment in Fox Hall. So . . . now you'll have two of us breathing down your necks! Seriously, having spent a great deal of time with you girls over the past months—both in and out of the classroom— Dan and I are truly impressed with how much each one of you has grown. We are proud to be your teachers.

Love,
Maggie Grayson

Dear Mars,

I have great news! Miss Grayson and Mr. Griffith are not leaving Alma after all! They are going to be right here! I really missed seeing you at the play. Do you think there might be some chance we can get together before school is over? I hope so! Anyway, let's keep writing.

Sincerely,
Shanon

Dear Shanon,

I could kick myself for missing my chance to see you at that play. I dropped in on a couple of the guys' rehearsals over at Ardsley, and they seemed pretty good. Williams was also kind of disappointed that I couldn't make it, but he understood about Adams's poetry reading. Hope you do, too. I've just started a study group called The Hogs. We sit around the lunchroom, reading poetry and chugging down bacon cheeseburgers. Maybe someday you can join us. All joking aside, I miss you.

oveLay,
arsMay

Dear Amy,
    Haven't heard from you in a while. I am coming to the States in a couple of months and would love to see you. Maybe we can meet at your house in New York. How are things with the pen pals and with Lisa? The last time you wrote, you two were having a tiff. How was your school play? Write soon.

Love,
Evon

Dear Evon,
    Thanks for asking if everything is okay. It is! And am I glad! For a while I didn't know what was going on in our suite. Lisa told me the other day that she had been really jealous and had almost broken up with Rob. Anyway, things seem to be great with them again and with us.
    The play was absolutely unbelievable! It may even have been a turning point for me in my identity. All I think about now is how I want to be a real professional singer. But first I have to finish school.
    I would love to see you again! I have already talked to my parents about having Lisa, Shanon, and Palmer to my house for a weekend. Maybe that will be the weekend that you come and we can all spend it together! Bring your roller

skates again when you visit and we'll go to Central Park.

Love,
Amy

Dear John,

This is a short letter to say again how much I enjoyed your poetry-reading rehearsal and to thank you for the pink flower you sent me by way of Rob. I still feel as if I'm floating on air. I wish we would do the play again someday so you could see it. Write soon.

Amy

Dear Amy,

Here is a poem for you. My dad came to the reading and liked it. I wish he could have met you.

Feeling proud
Amy—the afternoon you came to me, wearing
Red and that smile and those black jeans
Even though I was shaking in my boots
Wielding power—I was the star poet that day!
Early sunrise is nothing
Limp, cloudless weather compared to your
Liveliness!

Yours truly,
John

Dear Lisa,

What can I say? Except what I've always known . . . that you are an exceptional girl. No, strike that—you are an exceptional person. I feel very lucky to be writing letters to you. It is on to other things with me, now that the play is over. I felt kind of down for a few days, but I'm fine now.

It was such a high! I will probably not have the chance to be the lead in anything else for the rest of my life. I will always remember this time though. I will also always remember you and me after the show.

Love,
Rob

Dear Rob,
    Thanks for your nice letter. I hope we never stop writing. It's like having a long talk with somebody. When I was at home, I would talk to my mom. Now I talk to Shanon. But I also need to talk to you. And writing letters is a good way to do it. I won't forget the afternoon of the show either. A lot of things have happened in my life this semester. I've been going through a whole lot of changes—most of them good. Our almost breaking up and then getting together again was really important. A better word might be significant.
    I was thinking, we're really young. Who knows what will happen next year or the year after that? But whatever does happen, we'll always have the memory of our friendship in this first year that we became pen pals. I'll write to you next week. To me you'll always be Everyman.

Love,
Lisa

P.S. This letter comes sealed with a kiss!

P.S. Have you missed any Pen Pals? Catch up now!

PEN PALS #1: BOYS WANTED!

Suitemates Lisa, Shanon, Amy, and Palmer love the Alma Stephens School for Girls. There's only one problem—no boys! So the girls put an ad in the newspaper of the nearby Ardsley Academy for Boys asking for male pen pals. Soon their mailboxes are flooded with letters and photos from Ardsley boys, but the girls choose four boys from a suite just like their own. Through their letters, the girls learn a lot about their new pen pals—and about themselves.

PEN PALS #2: TOO CUTE FOR WORDS

Palmer, the rich girl from Florida, has never been one for playing by the rules. So when she wants Amy's pen pal, Simmie, instead of her own, she simply takes him. She writes to Simmie secretly and soon he stops writing to Amy. When Shanon, Lisa, and Amy find out why, the suite is in an uproar. How could Palmer be so deceitful? Before long,

Palmer is thinking of leaving the suite—and the other girls aren't about to stop her. Where will it all end?

PEN PALS #3: P.S. FORGET IT!

Palmer is out to prove that her pen pal is the best—and her suitemate Lisa's is a jerk. When Lisa receives strange letters and a mysterious prank gift, it looks as if Palmer may be right. But does she have to be so smug about it? Soon it's all-out war in Suite 3-D!

From the sidelines, Shanon and Amy think something fishy is going on. Is the pen pal scheme going too far? Will it stop before Lisa does something she may regret? Or will the girls learn to settle their differences?

PEN PALS #4: NO CREEPS NEED APPLY

Palmer takes up tennis so she can play in the Alma-Ardsley tennis tournament with her pen pal, Simmie Randolph III. Lisa helps coach Palmer, and soon Palmer has come so far that they are both proud of her. But when Palmer finds herself playing *against*—not *with*—her super-competitive pen pal, she realizes that winning the game could mean losing *him*!

Palmer wants to play her best, and her suitemates will think she's a real creep if she lets down the school. Is any boy worth the loss of her friends?

PEN PALS #5: SAM THE SHAM

Palmer has a new pen pal. His name is Sam O'Leary, and he seems absolutely perfect! Palmer is walking on air. She can't think or talk about anything but Sam—even when she's supposed to be tutoring Gabby, a third-grader from town, as part of the school's community-service requirement. Palmer thinks it's a drag, until she realizes just how much she means to little Gabby. And just in time, too—she needs something to distract her from her own problems when it appears that there *is* no Sam O'Leary at Ardsley. But if that's the truth—who *has* been writing to Palmer?

PEN PALS #6: AMY'S SONG

The Alma Stephens School is buzzing with excitement—the girls are going to London! Amy is most excited of all. She and her pen pal John have written a song together, and one of the Ardsley boys has arranged for her to sing it in a London club. It's the chance of a lifetime! But once in London, the girls are constantly supervised, and Amy can't see how she'll ever get away to the club. She and her suite-mates plot and scheme to get out from under the watchful eye of their chaperone, but it's harder than they thought it would be. It looks as if Amy will never get her big break!

PEN PALS #7: HANDLE WITH CARE

Shanon is tired of standing in Lisa's shadow. She wants to be thought of as her own person. So she decides to run for Student Council representative—against Lisa! Lisa not only feels abandoned by her best friend, but by her pen pal, too. While the election seems to be bringing Shanon and Mars closer together, it's definitely driving Lisa and Rob apart. Lisa's sure she'll win the election. After all, she's always been a leader—shy Shanon's the follower. Or is she? Will the election spoil the girls' friendship? And will it mean the end of Rob and Lisa?

PEN PALS #9: STOLEN PEN PALS

Shanon, Lisa, Amy, and Palmer have been very happy with their pen pals—but now they have competition! Four very preppy—and very pretty—girls from Brier Hall have advertised for Ardsley pen pals. And pen pals they get—including Rob, Mars, and John! Soon the boys are living at the rival school as part of an exchange program—and the Fox Hall suitemates' mailboxes are empty. The girls may have had their differences, but there's one thing they can agree on: Brier Hall must be stopped!

WANTED: BOYS — AND GIRLS —
WHO CAN WRITE !

Join the Pen Pals Exchange and get a pen pal of your own!
Fill out the form below.
Send it with a self-addressed stamped envelope to:

PEN PALS EXCHANGE
c/o The Trumpet Club
PO Box 632
Holmes, PA 19043
U.S.A.

In a couple of weeks you'll receive the name and address
of someone who wants to be your pen pal.

Cut here ---

PEN PALS EXCHANGE

NAME _____ GRADE _____

ADDRESS _____

TOWN _____ STATE _____ ZIP _____

DON'T FORGET TO INCLUDE A STAMPED ENVELOPE
WITH YOUR NAME AND ADDRESS ON IT!